SPECIAL MESSAGE TO READERS

This book is published under the auspices of

THE ULVERSCROFT FOUNDATION

(registered charity No. 264873 UK)

Established in 1972 to provide funds for research, diagnosis and treatment of eye diseases. Examples of contributions made are: —

A Children's Assessment Unit at Moorfield's Hospital, London.

•

Twin operating theatres at the Western Ophthalmic Hospital, London.

•

A Chair of Ophthalmology at the Royal Australian College of Ophthalmologists.

•

The Ulverscroft Children's Eye Unit at the Great Ormond Street Hospital For Sick Children, London.

You can help further the work of the Foundation by making a donation or leaving a legacy. Every contribution, no matter how small, is received with gratitude. Please write for details to:

THE ULVERSCROFT FOUNDATION,
The Green, Bradgate Road, Anstey,
Leicester LE7 7FU, England.
Telephone: (0116) 236 4325

In Australia write to:
THE ULVERSCROFT FOUNDATION,
c/o The Royal Australian and New Zealand
College of Ophthalmologists,
94-98 Chalmers Street, Surry Hills,
N.S.W. 2010, Australia

INSTANT FIRE

Joanna had never experienced any-thing like it before. As a civil engineer, working in a man's world, she'd never before felt the raw magnetism which drew her to Clay Thackeray. How-ever, whereas she loved him, he lusted after her — difference number one. Secondly, was it her, or her company shares he wanted? And finally, she didn't want to put on her apron, cook and take care of babies. They did say, 'Marry in haste . . . '

LIZ FIELDING

INSTANT FIRE

Complete and Unabridged

LINFORD
Leicester

First published in Great Britain in 1993

First Linford Edition
published 2010

Copyright © 1993 by Liz Fielding
All rights reserved

British Library CIP Data

Fielding, Liz.
    Instant fire. - - (Linford romance library)
    1. Women engineers- -Fiction.
    2. Love stories.
    3. Large type books.
    I. Title II. Series
    823.9′14–dc22

    ISBN 978–1–44480–181–1

Published by
F. A. Thorpe (Publishing)
Anstey, Leicestershire

Set by Words & Graphics Ltd.
Anstey, Leicestershire
Printed and bound in Great Britain by
T. J. International Ltd., Padstow, Cornwall

This book is printed on acid-free paper

1

There was an urgency about the ring and Joanna groaned. It was the first Saturday she hadn't worked in weeks and she had planned a lazy morning. She pulled on her dressing-gown. 'I'm coming,' she called, as there was a second peremptory burst on the bell.

The postman grinned as she opened the door. 'Sorry, Miss Grant, but this one needs signing for.' Jo took the recorded delivery letter and signed where the postman indicated. 'Thanks. You can go back to bed now.' She glared at his back, then turned the letter over. The envelope was thick. Nothing cheap about whoever sent the letter inside, she thought. She opened it and unfolded the single sheet. She read it quickly through and frowned. It was from a firm of solicitors offering to purchase, at a very good price indeed, a block of shares she had inherited from her father.

She read it through a second time. The purchaser was not named. 'A gentleman has instructed us . . . ' that was all. Jo shrugged and threw the letter on to her desk to answer later. It didn't matter who the 'gentleman' was. Her shares in Redmond Construction were not for sale.

*　*　*

'You, lad!'

Jo flung a contemptuous glance over the scaffolding. Another short-sighted idiot who assumed that because she was on a construction site she must be male. Nevertheless she inspected the figure standing in the yard with interest. He was leaning against a gunmetal-grey Aston Martin and despite the foreshortened angle she could see that he was well above average height. In fact, she thought, dressed in a beautifully cut lightweight tweed suit, he was an altogether impressive figure, and gave the disturbing impression that he wasn't short of anything.

'What do you want?' she called down.

He raised a hand to shade his eyes against a sudden shaft of sunlight breaking through the clouds.

'I'm looking for Joe Grant. Is he up there?' he called.

'I'll come down,' she shouted, swinging herself on to the first of a series of ladders to descend the fifty-odd feet to the ground and then turning to face the stranger. She had been right about his height. Despite owning to five feet ten inches in stockings she was forced to look up into the lean, weather-beaten face of a man whose very presence commanded attention. And into remarkable blue eyes which contrasted vividly with a pelt of black curly hair that no amount of the most expert cutting would ever quite keep under control. Blue eyes that were regarding her with puzzlement, as if he knew something wasn't right, but couldn't quite put his finger on what was bothering him.

The sudden rise in her pulse-rate at the sight of this tanned stranger, the heat that seared her cheekbones and parted her lips, an immediate recognition of some deep primeval need that he had stirred, shook her easy assurance.

She clamped her lips together. 'Well?' she demanded and her voice was shockingly sharp in her ears.

A slight frown creased his forehead. 'My name is Thackeray,' he said, his soft voice seeming to vibrate into her very bones. 'I'm looking for Joe Grant. A girl at the office told me he was working here.'

Jo stuck her hands deep in her pockets in an unconsciously boyish gesture and walked quickly away from him. 'You'd better come over to the site office, Mr Thackeray,' she looked back over her shoulder and called to him.

'I've been to the office already. He's not there.' He seemed reluctant to follow her.

'He will be.' Jo opened the door and waited. The man shrugged and moved after her and she went inside, removing her hard hat, enjoying the small triumph of satisfaction at the exclamation from behind her as a thick mop of dark blonde hair swung free to frame her face. She shrugged out of the ancient Barbour, several sizes too large, and turned to face him. 'I'm Jo Grant, Mr Thackeray. Now, what exactly can I do for you?'

A smile charged his eyes with warmth as he acknowledged his mistake. 'I can think of any number of things. Accept my most humble apologies, perhaps?'

'Perhaps,' she conceded, cloaking her heart's racketing response to his smile in cool politeness. This man had never been humble.

'Does it happen often?'

'Often enough. There's no reason for you to feel stupid.'

'Oh, I don't,' he said, easily. 'Dressed in an outsized jacket, wellingtons and a hard hat, even the most glamorous woman might be mistaken for a boy.'

His amusement was galling. And she hadn't missed the implication that since she wasn't glamorous it was perfectly reasonable for him to make such a mistake.

'Perhaps you would get to the point, Mr Thackeray?'

'The point, Miss Grant?'

'You were looking for me. You've found me.'

'Oh, the point!' The smile died on his lips and his expression became quite still. 'The point is this, Jo Grant. I came to ask the bearer of that name out to lunch. So? What do you say?'

Jo drew her brows together in genuine surprise. 'Lunch? Why on earth would you want to take me out to lunch.'

He looked at her more intently. 'You would find such an invitation surprising?' he asked. There was a certain practised charm about him and she realised, with a slight shock, that he was flirting with her.

'Of course I'm surprised. You don't know me.'

'True,' he conceded. 'And I have to own up to the fact that the Joe Grant I'm looking for weighs around fifteen stone, has a beard and is in his fifties. But I am very happy to accept you as his substitute.'

Jo sat down rather suddenly. 'No substitute at all, I'm afraid. But I'm the nearest you're going to get. My father is dead.'

'Joe's dead?' There was no disguising the shock in his voice. 'But he was no age.' He seemed genuinely upset and for a moment stared through the window. Then he looked down at her as if seeing her for the first time. 'You're Joe's daughter? The one in the picture on his desk?' He frowned. 'But you were all spectacles and braces.'

Jo remembered the dreadful picture in an old frame that had been almost buried among the clutter on her father's desk. 'Yes, I'm afraid I was. Poor Dad. I usually managed to avoid having my photograph taken, but that was a school job. There was no escape. Mum felt obliged to buy it but out of deference to my feelings she wouldn't put it next to my sister's.'

'Really? Why was that?'

'Heather has curls, straight teeth and twenty-twenty vision.' She shrugged. 'Dad took pity on me.'

Measuring blue eyes regarded her with provoking self-assurance. 'I'm certain you'd give your sister a run for her money these days, Miss Grant.'

She smiled slightly. 'I'm afraid not, Mr Thackeray. Heather is still the family beauty. I had to make do with the brains.'

'Poor you.'

Jo stiffened. 'I don't require sympathy, Mr Thackeray,' she blurted out, then coloured furiously at her stupid outburst as she saw the laughter lighting the depths of his eyes. This man was getting under her skin, breaking through the barriers she had erected as part of the price for her acceptance in a man's world.

'Your self-esteem still seems in need of a little propping up, if you don't mind my saying so. But I have to agree that you have no need of sympathy from me, or anyone else.' Before she could reply he had changed the subject. 'Joe said you planned to follow in his footsteps. I thought he was joking.'

'So did he, Mr Thackeray. By the time he realised his mistake it was too late to do anything about it.'

'Did he try?'

She remembered the pride on his face at her graduation, her mother's delight. 'Not very hard,' she assured him.

His look was thoughtful. 'I see.'

She had assumed he would take his leave once he had discovered that his errand was fruitless. Instead he folded himself into the chair at the side of her desk.

'I'm very sorry to hear about Joe's death, Miss Grant. What happened?' There was a genuine concern in his face which brought the old familiar ache to her throat. She stared hard at the schedules on the desk in front of her until the dangerous prickling behind her eyelids was under control.

'He was in his car. Apparently he had a heart attack.' Jo dragged her mind back to the present and looked up. 'It was three years ago.'

'I'm sorry. I didn't know. I've been overseas, working in Canada. I've been renewing some old acquaintances and when I phoned Redmonds' office to ask for your father they said — '

'It's all right. A simple mistake. It happens all the time; I should have learned to be less prickly by now.' She offered him her hand and a slightly rueful smile. 'Joanna Grant.'

His grasp was warm, the strong hand of a man you would want on your side. 'Clayton Thackeray.'

'Well, I'm sorry you had a wasted journey, Mr Thackeray.'

'Hardly wasted.' His eyes were intensely, disturbingly blue, and she looked hurriedly away.

'I'm not much of a substitute for Dad.'

'I liked and admired your father, Joanna. But it occurs to me that lunch with you will be every bit as enjoyable. And you're a great deal easier on the eye. Now that you've dispensed with the braces.'

'Don't be silly,' she protested. 'You don't have to take me . . . ' He waited, his face betraying nothing. 'I shouldn't . . . '

'Why not?' he asked.

'Because . . . ' There was no reason, apart from the fact that she wanted to go far too much for her own peace of mind.

He smiled as if he could see the battle taking place inside her head. 'Force yourself, Joanna.'

'I . . . ' He still had her hand firmly clasped in his much larger one. 'Thank you.' She found herself agreeing, without quite understanding why. Except that she didn't think he was the kind of man who ever took no for an answer.

'My pleasure. I booked a table at the

George on my way through the village. I'd planned to take your father there.'

'Did you? Then I'd better change my boots.' She put her head to one side and decided it was her turn to tease a little. 'But you don't have to impress me, Mr Thackeray. I'm just a site engineer. I usually have a sandwich down the pub.'

Laughter produced deep creases around his eyes and down his cheeks. 'I'm not looking for a job, Joanna. And my friends call me Clay. Do what you have to. I'll wait in the car.'

She kicked off her boots, slipped her feet into narrow low-heeled shoes and ran a clothes brush over her grey woollen trousers, wishing for once that she had a skirt to change into. Her soft cream shirt had been chosen more for comfort than style, but at least her sweater was a pretty, if impractical, mixture of pink and white. A gift from Heather, her older sister, who ran a stylish boutique and never ceased in her attempts to add a little femininity to

Jo's wardrobe which tended to run to hardwearing clothes suitable for the site. She took down the calendar that hid the mirror, her one concession to vanity in this male world, and regarded her reflection with disfavour.

Then she shrugged. 'Don't kid yourself, Jo,' she told herself sternly. 'He's taking you out to lunch because he knew your father. Don't get any silly ideas.' She pulled a face at herself, but nevertheless Heather would have been pleased to see how long her little sister spent on her hair and make-up.

Clay Thackeray ushered her into the car, opening the door and settling her comfortably before sliding into the driving seat. She was aware of interested eyes watching from every part of the site and knew that she would be teased mercilessly for the next few days by men opening doors with exaggerated politeness, offering her their arm on the scaffolding. They wouldn't miss a trick.

'It would be just the same if you were a man being picked up by a girl, you know. Probably worse.' He reversed the car and turned into the lane.

She laughed. 'Do you read minds for a living?'

'No, but I was a site engineer myself once.'

'Were you?' Jo gave him a sideways glance from under long, dark lashes. He'd come a long way from that lowly position. 'And I have no doubt that a great many girls picked you up.'

He turned and smiled. 'A few,' he admitted. 'And your father certainly knew how to tease.'

'Yes, he did.' She had worked on sites with him during the long summer holidays from university and she had seen him at work. Had been the butt of his jokes, too. The slightest mistake was ruthlessly exploited. She had hated it, but it had toughened her up. The Aston purred as he drove gently down the lane. 'This is a lovely car.'

'Yes, it was my father's. He hasn't driven it much in recent years but he wouldn't let me buy it from him until he considered I was old enough to be trusted with it.'

'And are you?'

'Thirty-three?' he offered. 'What do you think? The old man wanted to wait another year. He didn't have his first Aston until he was nearly thirty-five. But I forced his hand. I threatened to buy a BMW.' He turned into the George's car park.

'What a dreadful thing to do!' But the laughter in her voice softened the words.

'Wasn't it?' Their hands touched as he reached to unclip her seatbelt and they looked up at the same moment. For a long second Jo thought the world must have stopped spinning. 'I want to kiss you, Jo Grant.' His voice grated over a million tiny nerve-endings and she swallowed. Her pulse was hammering in her ears and she could hardly breathe. Girls weren't supposed to kiss men they had just met. They certainly weren't supposed to admit they wanted to.

Jo fought the inclination to meet him halfway and lifted one brow. 'And do you always get what you want, Clayton Thackeray?'

'Always,' he assured her.

Flustered by the unwavering certainty in his eyes, she made an effort at a laugh. 'Really, Mr Thackeray, I thought the form was that you wine and dine a girl before you make a pass,' she said, attempting to hide her bewildering, unexpected hunger for this man, bury it under a flippancy she was far from feeling.

Clay Thackeray stared at her for a moment, then he released the seatbelt, making her jump, breaking the spell. 'You're right, of course. And this is only lunch. I'll have to give some thought to the question of dinner.'

Before she could gather her wits he was opening the car door for her. His hand under her arm seemed to burn through the sleeve of her jacket and neither of them spoke as he led her inside the restaurant. Clay caught the eye of the waiter and they were shown straight to their table in the corner, overlooking the river.

Jo kept her eyes firmly on the view from the window, anything but face the man opposite. She spent her working life with men and they rarely managed to find her at a loss for a word. But right now she couldn't think of a thing to say. At least nothing that made any sense.

No such problem tormented Clay. 'Let me see if I can read your thoughts again,' he suggested. Jo's grey eyes widened. The disturbing thoughts racing unbidden through her mind were not the kind she wanted him to read. 'Duck?' he said softly, a suspicion of laughter in his voice.

'Is that an instruction or an observation?' she asked, making a supreme effort to keep the atmosphere light.

'An observation,' he replied, drily, pointing to the birds on the riverbank. 'You seem to be fascinated by them; I thought perhaps you were deciding which one you wanted for lunch.' He offered her the menu. 'Or perhaps you'd rather run an eye over this?'

Jo buried her face in the menu and by the time the waiter returned to take their order had regained something of her natural composure.

'Something to drink?'

'A pineapple juice topped up with soda, please.'

Clay relayed this request to the waiter and added a mineral water for himself.

'You said you have just come back from Canada?' Jo asked, leading the conversation into neutral territory. 'What were you doing there?'

'Working. My mother was a French Canadian. When she died I realised how little I knew about her or where she came from. I wanted to find out.'

'And now you're having a holiday?'

He hesitated for a moment before he said, 'Not exactly. But I'm looking up old friends. When the receptionist at Redmonds said Joe was working here it was close enough to home to take a chance on finding him at the site.'

'Home?' She tried to ignore the treacherous rise in her pulse-rate at the thought of him living near by.

'I bought a cottage on the river at Camley when I was over at Christmas.'

He was staying, and she was ridiculously, stupidly pleased. 'I love Camley. It's so unspoilt.' She was babbling, but he seemed not to notice.

'Yes. It's the reason I bought the place.' He pulled a face. 'Stupid, really. My offices are in London; a service flat would be a lot less bother. But I couldn't resist the cottage. It's old and it needs a lot of work, but I suppose that was part of its charm. The builder has finished putting the structure to rights and it's habitable, but I'm just camping there at the moment.'

'So you're not going back to Canada?'

'Not permanently. At least for the foreseeable future.' He regarded her with steady amusement. 'Are you pleased?' he asked.

The arrival of the waiter saved her from the embarrassment of a reply and she regarded the poached salmon he placed before her with a sudden loathing for its pinkness . . . the same colour that she was only too aware was staining her cheeks.

'Hollandaise?' Forced to look up, she discovered that he wasn't laughing at her as she had suspected. His smile was unexpectedly warm. 'I am,' he said. 'Very pleased.'

She swallowed and took the dish he offered. 'Did you work with Dad for long?' she asked, the catch in her voice barely noticeable.

'He was my first project manager. I came to Redmonds from university and was put to work under him. I was very fortunate. You must miss him.'

'Yes, I miss him. I wanted him to . . . ' Her voice trailed away. That was too private a need to be shared. Not something to be spoken aloud.

Sensitive to the fact that he had strayed into dangerous territory, he changed the subject, describing his life in Canada, the country. On safer ground, Jo at last began to relax.

When coffee arrived he sat back in his chair and regarded her seriously. 'So what are your career plans, Joanna? Surely you don't intend to stay on site?'

'I was the first woman that Redmonds employed as a site engineer,' she said, with a certain pride. 'I plan to be the first woman they appoint as a project manager.'

If he was surprised he hid it well enough, but his next question suggested that he had some understanding of the problems involved. 'Does that leave you any room for a personal life?'

'Not much,' she admitted.

'But what about marriage? Raising a family?'

'Men manage to have both.' She was no stranger to this argument. Her sister had tried so many times to persuade her to take up a more conventional career that she had once offered to make a tape recording and play it at least once a day to save her the bother. But Heather had long since stopped trying to change her and confined her efforts these days to improving her wardrobe.

'True, and probably not very fair. But men don't get pregnant. Climbing up and down ladders might get to be a bit of a problem, don't you think?'

Since Jo had no intention of getting pregnant in the foreseeable future, she ignored the question and glanced at her watch. 'It's late. I should get back.'

Clay regarded her thoughtfully for a moment, but didn't pursue the subject. Instead he summoned the waiter and asked for the bill. 'Now, about dinner. Where shall I pick you up?'

Surprise that he should want to see her again made her laugh a little uncertainly. 'There's no need, Clay, really. It was very kind of you to take me out to lunch, but — '

'I didn't bring you here to be kind.' He leaned forward. 'I still want to kiss you, Jo Grant. You were the one who stipulated being wined and dined first. Of course, perhaps you've changed your mind.' His eyes glinted wickedly. 'In which case I'll be happy to oblige right now.'

'I didn't . . . ' Joanna bit back the denial and stood up. It was a ridiculous conversation and she had no intention of prolonging it. Clay rose and she smiled, graciously, she hoped. 'Please don't let me rush you.' She offered Clay her hand and he shook it solemnly. 'Thank you for lunch. I won't trouble you for a lift. I can get a taxi back to work.' She moved swiftly across the dining-room, making for the pay-phone in Reception, where she searched furiously in her bag.

'Can I offer you some change?' He was leaning against the wall, watching her.

'No, thank you,' Jo said coldly. Then, as she realised that she had none, she changed her mind. 'Yes,' she snapped.

'It'll be at least ten minutes before one comes,' Clay said, gently, offering her a handful of silver coins. 'Why don't you want me to take you?'

She refused to meet his eye. Selecting a ten-pence coin, Jo fiercely punched in the number of the local taxi service listed by the phone.

'Don't you want me to kiss you?' he asked, seriously. 'I rather thought you did.'

The phone was ringing in her ear. 'Keble Taxis, how can I help you?'

'I should like a taxi to collect me from the George as quickly as possible, please,' Jo said, studiously ignoring the man at her side.

'We're rather busy at the moment,' the girl told her. 'It'll be twenty minutes.'

'Twenty minutes!'

Clay took the phone from her hand and spoke into the receiver. 'We'll leave it, thank you.' He hung up. 'I can't have you late for work, can I? Not a dedicated career-woman like you. You'll be quite safe, I promise.'

Before she could protest further he had opened the door and swept her towards the car. Settled against the worn leather, Jo was aware of a certain breathlessness. On site, except for visits from the project manager, she was in control. But she had somehow lost that control when Clay Thackeray had walked into her office. The word safe was completely inappropriate. He was a dangerously disturbing man.

They didn't speak as they sped along the country lanes and it was with a certain relief that Jo saw the site earthworks appear above the hedge. Clay pulled into the yard and stopped. She tried to escape but he was faster, catching her hand as she moved to release the seatbelt, holding it against his chest so that she could feel the steady thudding of his heart.

'Now you have to decide, Jo Grant.'

Jo glared at him. 'You promised!'

'Did I?' He challenged her softly. 'I remember saying that you would be safe. I didn't specify what I would keep you safe from.'

How could such open, honest eyes

hide such a devious nature? she fumed. 'In that case I'll get it over with now, if it's all the same to you.' Ignoring the fact that they had the rapt attention of the site staff, she closed her eyes and waited. A soft chuckle made her open them again. Clay was shaking his head.

'Round one to you, ma'am. On points.' He leaned across and pushed open the door for her. For a moment she sat, completely nonplussed. 'Well? Are you going to sit there all afternoon? I thought you were in a hurry.'

'Yes.' She made an effort to pull herself together. 'Thank you again for lunch,' she said, automatically.

She climbed from the car and walked quickly across to her office, firmly refusing to give in to the impulse to look back.

★　★　★

It was Thursday before he phoned. A whole week.

'Joanna?' Her heart skipped a beat as

the low voice spoke her name.

'Clay?' she echoed the query in his voice, but ruefully acknowledged that the man knew how to play the game. She had been on tenterhooks all week, expecting him to turn up at the site every moment. The mere glimpse of a grey car was enough to send her heart on a roller-coaster. But he hadn't come and she had called herself every kind of fool for refusing his invitation to dinner. And then called herself every kind of fool for wanting to get involved with him. He was completely out of her reach. She hadn't the experience to cope with such a man. She hadn't the experience, full stop.

'How are you, Joanna?' She could almost see the cool amusement in those eyes.

'Fine, thank you. And you? Are you enjoying your holiday?'

'Not much. I've been in the Midlands all week on business. But you could change all that. Have dinner with me tonight.'

'Have all your old girlfriends got married while you've been away?' she parried, a little breathlessly, not wishing to seem too eager.

He chuckled. 'Most of them. It has been nearly seven years. Will you come?'

'I . . . ' For a moment there was war between desire and common sense. Desire had no competition. 'I'd love to.'

2

It was late when Jo finally parked the car behind the old house in the nearby market town of Woodhurst. She let herself into the first-floor flat that she had rented for the duration of the job and dumped her shopping on the kitchen table.

She wasted very little time in the shower and quickly dried her hair, a thick, dark blonde mop, streaked with pale highlights from so much time spent out of doors. There had been a time when she had wondered what it would be like to have curls like her sister, but had long since accepted the fact that they weren't for her. Her nose was a little too bold and her mouth overlarge. Curls, a kindly hairdresser had told the fourteen-year-old Joanna as he'd cut away the disastrous results of Heather's attempt to provide the missing locks with a home perm, were for those girls whose face lacked character. She hadn't believed him, even then, but these days she was content with a style that needed little more than a cut once every three weeks to keep it looking good.

Satisfied with her hair, she spent a great deal longer than usual on her make-up and painted her nails pale pink. Tonight she was determined to be Joanna Grant. Jo the site engineer could, for once, take a back seat.

She had few evening clothes and she hadn't needed to deliberate on what she would wear. She stepped into a floating circle of a skirt in pale grey georgette and topped it with a long-sleeved jacket in toning greys and pinks with a touch of silver thread in the design. She fastened large pale pink circles of agate twisted around with silver to her ears and regarded the result with a certain satisfaction. It was quite possible, she thought, with some amusement, that, in the unlikely event they should bump into any of her colleagues tonight, they would be hard pressed to recognise her.

Slipping her feet into low-heeled grey pumps, Jo spun in front of her mirror, coming to a sudden halt at the sound of her doorbell. She stood for a moment, as if rooted to the spot, vulnerable, uncertain of herself. Then the fear that he might not wait lent wings to her heels as she flew to the door.

Clay, his tall figure a study in elegance in the stark blackness of a dinner-jacket, was leaning against the stairpost regarding the toe of his shoe, and he glanced up as she flung open the door. He started to smile and then stopped, cloaking the expression in his eyes as he straightened and stared at the girl framed in the doorway.

'Are those for me?' Jo asked finally, to break the silence.

He glanced down at a spray of pink roses as if he couldn't think where they had come from, then back at her.

'I rather think they must be.'

'Come in. I'll put them in some water. Would you like a drink?' she asked, trying to remember what she had done with a bottle of sherry left over from Christmas.

'No, thanks.' He followed her into the cramped kitchen and watched as she clipped the stems and stood them in deep water to drink.

She turned to him. 'These are lovely, Clay. Thank you.'

'So are you, Joanna. No one would ever mistake you for a boy tonight.' He took a step towards her then turned away, raking long fingers through his hair. 'I think we had better go.' For the briefest moment it had seemed as if he was going to kiss her, and the thought quickened her blood, sending it crazily through her veins. Instead he opened the door and she followed him down the stairs to the waiting taxi.

'Where are we going?' she asked.

'A little place I know by the river.' This deprecating description hardly did justice to the elegant restaurant overlooking the Thames and she told him so.

'I thought you would like to come here.' He seemed oddly distracted.

'It's beautiful.'

He turned and looked down at her. 'Yes. It is.' He lifted his hand to her cheek, his fingertips lingering against the smooth perfection of her skin. 'Quite beautiful.'

'May I show you to your table, sir?'

Clay dragged himself back from wherever his thoughts had taken him and he tucked his arm under Joanna's. They made a striking couple as they walked across the restaurant and several heads turned to follow their progress. Joanna was usually forced to disguise her height when walking with a man, never wearing high heels and, if not exactly slumping, at least keeping what her father had laughingly described as a very relaxed posture. Now, beside the strong figure of Clay Thackeray, the top of her head just reaching his ear, she stretched to her full height, human enough to enjoy the knowledge that she was envied by at least half the women present. Probably more.

Afterwards she couldn't have described anything they had eaten or much of what they had talked about, although she thought he had told her something about a consultancy that he had begun in Canada and his plans for expansion into Britain. All she could remember was Clay's face in the candlelight, his hand reaching for hers across the table, the words, 'Let's go home.'

In the back of the car she curled against him as if she had known him for years. His arm drew her close and it seemed the most natural thing in the world to rest her head on his shoulder. She didn't think about where they were going. She didn't care, as long as he held her.

The car eventually stopped and she lifted her head. 'Where are we?' she asked.

'You are home, fair lady. Where did you expect to be?'

Glad of the darkness to hide her blushes, she allowed him to help her from the car.

'I'll see you to your door.'

She turned to him at the top of the stairs. 'Would you like a coffee?'

'I think I'm going to have enough trouble sleeping, Jo.' His arm was around her waist and she didn't ever want him to let go of her. As if reading her mind, he pulled her closer. 'But, before I go, I believe you promised me a kiss.'

She lowered her eyes, suddenly shy. 'Now?' she asked.

'Now,' he affirmed, and his lips touched hers for the briefest moment, the time it took her heart to beat. He drew back the space of an inch, no more. 'Joanna?' His voice was a question and an answer. Then his mouth descended upon hers and her willing response answered any question he cared to ask.

When at last he released her she could hardly support herself, and he held her in the circle of his arms and stood for a moment with her head upon his shoulder.

'I must go.'

'Must you?'

'Don't make it any harder.' He kissed the top of her head and she looked up, but he seemed to be far away, no longer with her. She fumbled in her bag for her key and he took it from her and opened the door.

'Can I see you tomorrow?'

She hesitated for a moment, but then he smiled and on a catch of breath she nodded. 'Yes.'

He raised his hand briefly. 'I'll pick you up at seven.' Then he was gone without a backward glance and for the first time in her life she felt the pain of being torn in two. Her other half had walked down the stairs in the palm of Clay Thackeray's hand.

★ ★ ★

Joanna wondered briefly, as she stood under a reviving shower, exactly what she had thought about before the appearance of Clay Thackeray. Since his appearance a week earlier he had filled her waking hours completely, and a good few of her sleeping ones.

A ring at the door put a stop to these thoughts and she grabbed a towelling wrap and went to answer it.

'Clay!'

'I'm a little early,' he apologised.

'Just a little,' she agreed, laughter dancing in her eyes. 'I thought we were meeting at seven p.m., not seven a.m.'

'I had this sudden yearning to know what you looked like first thing in the morning.' His eyes drifted down the deep V of her wrap and she grabbed self-consciously at it and tightened the belt, feeling at something of a disadvantage alongside the immaculate dark blue pin-striped suit and stark white shirt.

'Well?'

'Exactly as I imagined. No make-up, bare feet, hair damp from the shower . . . ' she lifted her hand self-consciously, but he anticipated the move and caught her fingers ' . . . and quite beautiful.' He stepped through the door and closed it firmly behind him.

She laughed a little nervously and stepped back in the face of such assured advances. 'Compliments so early in the morning deserve some reward. Would you like some breakfast?'

One stride brought him to her side. He slid an arm around her waist and drew her close. 'That, sweet Joanna, rather depends upon the menu.'

Jo's breathing was a little ragged. 'Eggs?' she heard herself say. He made no response. 'I might have some bacon.' His eyes never left hers. 'Toast?' she offered, desperately. 'I haven't much time. I have to get to . . . ' He leaned forward and brushed his lips against hers and she no longer cared about the time.

'You, Jo. Don't you know that I want you for breakfast?'

He pulled the knot of her wrap and she made no move to stop him. Last night she knew that with very little persuasion she would have fallen into bed with him. He had known that too. It had been far too easy to fall in love with him. In the long, wakeful hours of the night she had determined that this evening she would put on some emotional armour along with her make-up. But, almost as if he had anticipated this, he had outmanoeuvred her, taking her by surprise with this early-morning raid. No make-up. No armour. No clothes. The harsh ring of the doorbell made her jump and he straightened, a crooked smile twisting his mouth.

'Saved by the bell, Jo.' For a moment he held the edges of her robe, then he pulled it close around her and retied the knot before standing aside for her to open the door.

'Sorry, Miss Grant. Another of those recorded delivery letters for you to sign. You'd better pay up!' She smiled automatically at the postman's bantering humour and signed the form. This time she didn't bother to open the letter, but threw it on the hall table.

'Aren't you going to open it?' Clay asked. 'It looks urgent.'

'I know what it says. It's from someone who wants to buy some shares I own. I've already told them I won't sell.'

'Oh? Maybe they've increased their offer.'

She frowned. 'Do you think so? I wonder why they want them?' Her eyes lingered for a moment on the envelope. 'Perhaps I ought to find out — '

'Forget them! They're not important.' She lifted her eyes to his and all thoughts of shares were driven from her head as he kissed her once more. But the moment of madness had passed and when he finally raised his head she took an unsteady step back.

'I really must get ready for work, Clay.'

'Must you?' He frowned, then shrugged. 'Of course you must. And I'm delaying you.' He turned for the door.

'Clay, why did you come here this morning?'

He paused for a moment, his

knuckles white as he gripped the door-handle, as if debating with himself. When he looked back it was with a deadly and earnest force. 'I thought we might have dinner at the cottage tonight,' he said. His eyes were unreadable.

She didn't stop to think. It was already far too late for thinking. 'I'd love to,' she said, the words barely escaping her throat.

She stood in the hall for a long moment after he had left, then, gathering her wits, she turned to get ready for work. Her eyes fell on the letter and impatiently she tore it open. Clay had been right, the offer had indeed been increased. His apparent omniscience gave her a ridiculous burst of pleasure.

★　★　★

Clay arrived on the stroke of seven and Jo picked up the soft leather bag that held everything she might need. She locked the door behind them and opened her bag to drop in the key, then turned to see him watching her.

'Got everything?' he asked.

'Yes, thank you.' Her cheeks were warm as she turned to follow him down the stairs to the waiting car.

The cottage was beautiful and very old, built of narrow autumn-coloured bricks, with a drunken pantile roof where a pair of fantail doves, golden in the evening light, were flirting. The garden had been neglected, but already work had begun to restore the stone pathways and a dilapidated dovecote. He helped her out of the car and for a moment she just stood and took it all in.

'It's lovely.'

'I'm glad you like it. Come and see what I've been doing inside.' Her heart was hammering as he led her up the path and opened the door, standing back to let her step across the threshold and into the hall.

The floor had been newly stripped

and re-polished and a jewel-rich Persian rug lay before them. She dropped her bag at the bottom of the stairs.

'Hungry?' he asked.

She shook her head. 'Not very. Will you show me round?'

'The grand tour?' He laughed. 'It won't take very long.'

The colour in her cheeks deepened slightly. She just needed a little time to gain her bearings. It would have been so much easier if they had gone out somewhere first. Good food, wine, eased the way.

'This is the study.' His voice made her jump. He opened a door on the left and led the way into a square room littered with wallpaper off-cuts. 'I've been trying to decide which paper to use.'

Glad of something positive to think about, Jo picked up various samples and held them against the wall. 'I like this one,' she said, finally.

'That's settled, then.'

She spun around. 'But . . . it's your choice.'

'Yes. I know.' He held the door to let her through. 'That's the cloakroom. Storage cupboard,' he said carelessly, as they passed closed doors. 'And this is the morning-room.'

'This is a cottage on a rather grand scale,' she said, admiring the use of yellow and white that would reflect the morning sun. She walked across to a pair of casement windows and opened them, stepping out into the garden. 'You're on the river!' she exclaimed. 'I hadn't realised.' She walked quickly down to the small mooring with its tiny dock.

'There's a boathouse behind those shrubs, but the roof has collapsed.'

'Will you rebuild it?'

'Maybe. Is it warm enough to eat out here, do you think?'

'Oh, yes! I've a sweater in my bag.' Once again the betraying heat stained her cheeks at this reminder.

'Go and get it while I organise the food.'

'You haven't finished the guided tour,' she said quickly. Then wished she hadn't.

'We've the whole evening. Don't be so impatient, Joanna. You'll see everything, I promise.'

She stood for long moments in the hall, making an effort to bring her breathing back under control. It was idiotic to be so jumpy. She was grown up. Twenty-four years old. She found the cloakroom and splashed cold water on to her face. Her eyes seemed twice their normal size in the mirror, the grey abnormally dark. 'Come on, Jo,' she told her reflection. 'You want this man so much it hurts.' If only he would make love to her, all her nerves would be swept away. But it was almost as if he was going out of his way not to touch her.

He had spread a cloth under a willow tree, its curtain providing a cloak of privacy from the passing boats, and was uncorking a bottle.

'Mrs Johnson has done us proud,' he said, as she settled on the rug beside him.

'Mrs Johnson?'

'She cooks, cleans, looks after me like a mother hen.'

'Oh.' Jo wasn't sure she liked the idea of an unknown woman cooking a seduction feast, wondering how many times she had done it before.

He handed her a glass of wine and touched the rim with his own. 'To Love.'

'Love — ?'

''You must sit down,' says Love, 'and taste my meat.' So I did sit and eat.'' He solemnly offered her a crab bouchée.

She quickly took one, but it seemed to fill her mouth and stick there. He topped up her glass and she drank nervously. For a moment he watched her, then he toyed with his food.

'How's Charles Redmond these days?'

'Charles?' She frowned. 'Of course, you must know him. He's made a good recovery by all accounts.'

'Will he retire, do you think?'

'I doubt it. The company is his life.' She was so glad of something ordinary to talk about, she didn't stop to consider that her boss was a very odd topic of conversation in the circumstances. She even began to enjoy the food. At last, though, the late May sun had dipped behind the trees and the temperature dropped sharply.

'Come on, you're shivering. I've kept you out here far too long.' He caught her around the waist and hurried her indoors. 'This way.' Clay led the way through a door to the right and turned on a lamp which softly illuminated the drawing-room. The floor was richly carpeted in Wedgwood-blue and a large, comfortable sofa was set square before the fireplace. Behind it stood an eighteenth-century sofa table. A well-rubbed leather wing-chair flanked the hearth. The only modern touch was the hi-fi equipment tucked away in an alcove. He bent and put a match to the fire. 'Warm yourself. I won't be a moment.'

Jo stood in front of the large open brick fireplace, watching the flames lick around the logs, wondering, with a sudden attack of nerves, if she was being an absolute fool. She had prided herself on her detachment, her ability to hold herself aloof from the idiotic disenchantment and pain she had seen her friends put themselves through. She had her job, her career to keep her content. Now here she was, in danger of falling into the same dangerous trap.

'Joanna?' His voice pulled her back to him and she understood then, as they stood side by side in the flickering firelight, just why people made such fools of themselves. Clay solemnly handed two glasses to her and, not once taking his eyes from hers, opened a bottle of champagne and allowed the golden bubbles to foam into them.

He raised his glass in silent homage to her. Jo sipped the champagne, hardly conscious of the bubbles prickling her tongue; only the heightened sensation of expectancy seemed real. The tiny nerve-endings in her skin were all at attention, tingling with nervous excitement, and quite suddenly she was shaking. Clay rescued her glass and stood it on the great wooden beam that formed the mantel.

He drew her into his arms, moulding her against his body, his eyes hooded with desire. 'I want you, Joanna Grant,' he said, and his voice stroked her softly. She leaned her head back slightly and smiled up at him, her self-possession a paper-thin veneer masking the ridiculous racketing of her heart, and as his lips touched hers she closed her eyes.

She thought she knew what it was like to be kissed by Clay Thackeray. Perhaps it was the champagne, or perhaps it was just that she had been anticipating this moment all day. For a few moments his wide, teasing mouth touched hers in a gentle exploration of the possibilities. Then he paused and she opened her eyes, parting her lips in an involuntary sigh as old as time, any lingering doubts having long since evaporated in the heat beating through her veins. He kissed her again, fleetingly, his eyes locked on to hers, then swung her into his arms and carried her to the sofa, sitting with her across his lap, her arms around his neck. For a moment his gaze focused on her mouth. Gently he outlined her lips with the tip of his finger. She moved urgently against him and whispered his name.

'Patience, my love. I want to enjoy you. Every bit of you.'

He peeled away her sweater, but his fingers were almost unbearably slow as they undid the buttons of her blouse and pushed the heavy cream silk aside. He kissed the soft mound of her breast where it swelled above her bra, then, edging the lace away, his mouth sought the hard peak of her nipple and she cried out as he drew it between his teeth and caressed it delicately with his tongue. Her breathing was ragged and there was a throbbing, desperate ache between her thighs which was strange and wonderful and which she was woman enough to know that only he could ease.

Her fingers dug into his shoulders.

'Clay . . . ' Her voice was pleading.

He raised his head and frowned slightly. 'Have all your lovers been so hurried?'

'No . . . ' But he wanted no answer; his mouth began a thorough and systematic plunder of hers, preventing her attempts to explain, then driving them out of her head altogether.

After a while he raised his head. 'I think it's time we went to bed.'

She raised lids heavy with desire and with her fingertips traced the strong line of his jaw and the small V-shaped scar on his chin. She drew her brows together in concentration. 'Clay . . . ' He caught her fingers, kissing each one in turn as she struggled to sit up. 'You should know . . . that is, I think I'd better tell you that I haven't ever — '

'Haven't what?' His mouth continued to caress her fingers and for a moment there was only silence in the flickering firelight. Then he realised that she had ceased to respond and he raised his head. 'What is it?'

'It was nothing important, Clay.' She tried to keep her voice light, conversational, but to her own ears failed dismally.

'You picked a hell of a moment to play games, sweetheart.' There was a slight edge to his voice. 'If you've got cold feet you only have to say.'

'No.' She threw him a desperate look. 'I just wanted you to know. That's all. I wanted you to know that I'm . . . ' She cleared her throat. 'I haven't . . . ' Why was the word so difficult to say? It was nothing to be ashamed of, after all. It just seemed silly. But surely by now he must understand what she was trying to tell him. Why on earth was he being so *slow*?

He was staring at her, a slight frown creasing the space between his brows. 'Joanna Grant,' he said at last, 'are you trying to tell me that you've never done this before?' She nodded, her face hot with embarrassment. 'That you're twenty-four years old and still a virgin?'

'There's no need to repeat yourself,'

Joanna said, fiercely proud. 'I'm well aware how ridiculous I must seem.'

'I . . . ' He seemed for a moment quite unable to speak, then he lifted her on to the sofa and stood up. 'Hardly ridiculous. But unexpected. To say the very least.'

She stood up, then, horribly, embarrassingly conscious of her state of undress, turned her back on him to straighten her clothes. She couldn't understand why it took so long, hardly aware how her fingers were trembling on the buttons. Finally, though, it was done. Pale and empty, she forced herself to face him.

'Could I ring for a taxi?' she asked, with as much dignity as she could muster. 'I think I should go home now.'

'I'm sorry, Joanna.' His regret sounded genuine enough, as well it might, she thought. He looked almost angry. 'I just hadn't anticipated this situation. Most of the women I've known are rather more — '

'You don't have to draw a picture, Clay.'

She should have known. He was used to sophisticated women who knew exactly how to please a man. Why had she ever thought he might be interested in her? Except that he had been, until she had been stupid enough to own up to her virgin state. It wasn't as if she wanted it. There had just been so many other things, important things she had to do.

She fled to the cloakroom. Like the other rooms she had seen, it had been gutted, and there was the smell of fresh plaster. The fittings were starkly new, but the tiles were still in their boxes, stacked against the wall, and the floor was bare board. He'd only just moved in. 'Camping' was the word he'd used. The quality of the fittings gave the word a slightly surrealistic edge. Not that it mattered.

She regarded herself in the mirror. Her cheeks were flushed and her lips red and swollen. She sighed and opened her bag to repair the damage as best she could.

Her sister had once suggested, quite kindly, that virginity beyond the age of twenty was an embarrassment she should try to resolve as quickly as possible. Apparently she had been right, but just now she didn't feel much like telling her so.

Clay was waiting when she emerged. He crossed the hall quickly to take her hand but she avoided his touch. 'Is there a telephone?'

'You don't have to go, Joanna. Can we talk?'

'Talk?' What on earth was there to talk about? she wondered. She hadn't come to talk. Her chin high, she turned away from him before she weakened. 'I'd prefer it if you would call a taxi.'

'Damn your taxi!' He reached for her.

'Now, Clay!' she demanded. If she let him touch her she would lose her hard-won self-control and simply weep.

For a moment the tension held him in suspension, neck muscles knotted into cords, hands clenched. Then, as if he had made a decision, he nodded slightly and relaxed.

'Perhaps you're right. Now is not the time. I'll take you home.'

'There's no need to put yourself to the trouble.'

'There's every need, Joanna. Don't argue.'

She made no further objection, sensing that it would be pointless, but she shook away his steadying hand at her elbow as she stumbled on the uneven path in the gathering darkness.

He insisted on seeing her to the door. She unlocked it and with a supreme effort managed a smile as she turned to face him.

'Goodbye, Clay.' She offered him her hand, sure now that she was safe. His expression grave, he took it, holding it for a moment as if he would say something. But he didn't speak. Instead he raised her fingers to his lips.

Before she could recover from her surprise he had turned and disappeared down the stairs. She ran to the front window in time to see the car door slam. It remained at the kerb for so long that she began to think he might get out again, but then, very quietly, the car pulled away and disappeared down the street.

No longer needing to keep a rigid control upon her feelings, she let out a long, shuddering sob.

⋆ ⋆ ⋆

Monday was a bad day at work, but Jo welcomed the problems. It used all her energies, blocked the need to think. She had spent the weekend with her sister, avoiding thinking, for once welcoming the disapproval of the long hours she worked, the unsuitable job. Thinking wouldn't do. She had made an utter fool of herself over Clay Thackeray and she would have to live with the memory of her humiliation for a very long time, but the longer she could put off thinking about it, the better.

'Good morning, Jo.'

Her heart sank. A visit from the project manager was the last thing she needed this morning. She turned to the sleek, tanned figure and forced a smile to her lips.

'Hello, Peter. We didn't expect you back until tomorrow. Had a good holiday?'

'Wonderful, my dear. The Greek islands in May are a perfect joy. You should have come with me.' He didn't exactly leer; he was never quite that obvious. But he hid his resentment at being landed with a woman on his site under a surface skim of flirtation that grated like a nail on a blackboard.

She shrugged and sighed. 'Someone has to stay and do the work. And I'm sure the company of your wife was adequate compensation. Do you want me to walk around with you?'

'No, it's nearly lunchtime. I've just come to take you all down the pub for a drink. A thank-you for all your hard work while I've been away. I'll give you a lift.' He placed his hand on her elbow and steered her towards his car.

Jo bit down hard to prevent herself from screaming. Not that he ever did anything that could be grounds for complaint. Just the innuendo and the proprietorial hand to her back, whenever there was anyone to see, to give the impression that she belonged to him personally.

Jo made for a table by the fireplace, but he moved her on to a secluded corner. 'It'll get noisy there when the place fills up.'

She fumed while he fetched the drinks. It wasn't as if he was interested in her, and for that at least she supposed she should be grateful. He was only interested in having the world believe that she was besotted by him.

'Now, my dear. Tell me everything that's happened while I've been away. Any problems?'

'Nothing major.' She smiled. 'You should have had another week in Greece.' The sentiment was heartfelt.

He leaned closer and placed his hand

on hers. 'I couldn't stay away that long.'

She looked up with relief as she heard the door opening in the corner. It would be the men from the site. But it wasn't them. Clay Thackeray stood framed in the doorway, very still, taking in the picture the two of them presented. For a moment their eyes clashed, then Clay took a step forward, his face taut with anger.

Quite deliberately Jo turned to Peter and smiled into his startled eyes. 'I'm glad. I've missed you, darling.' She leaned forward and kissed him lightly on the mouth.

His reaction should have been comic. It was a moot point who jumped most visibly — Peter, leaping to his feet, or Jo, at the crash of the door rattling on its hinges.

* * *

It was late when she drove home. The truth of the matter was that she didn't want to go back to her empty flat. At least while she was working she had something else to think about. Finally, however, the figures began to swim in front of her eyes and she was in danger of falling asleep over her desk. She parked the silver Mini in her allotted space and walked slowly up the stairs.

She was near the top when she became aware of an obstruction, and for a moment she stared uncomprehendingly at the long legs barring her way.

'You're very late. It's nearly nine o'clock.' Clay's voice was accusing.

She glanced at her watch. Anywhere to hide her face, to hide from him the betraying leap of joy at seeing him again. 'I've been working late.'

'I saw you working, at lunchtime.' His jaw muscles tightened. 'Who was he?'

It was too late to regret her stupidity. She had behaved very badly indeed and had the unhappy suspicion that Peter would make her pay for that when he had got over the shock. But it wasn't too late to retrieve a little self-respect.

'What's the matter, Clay? Did you change your mind?'

He stood up. 'This is hardly the place to discuss it.'

'This is the only place you're going to discuss anything. Because I have.' She turned away so that her eyes shouldn't betray the lie.

'Are you really so fickle?' He descended to her level and grasped her face between his hands so that she was forced to look at him. 'Who was he?' For a moment she glared furiously up at him, defying him to make her speak. He leaned closer. 'Who was he, Joanna?' he repeated, the velvet drawl of his voice contradicting the gem-hard challenge in his eyes.

'Peter Lloyd. He's the project manager.' The muscles in his jaw tightened and she closed her eyes. 'He's just come back from holiday.'

'You appeared to be very pleased to see him.'

'Did I? Maybe I was, Clay.'

'Maybe.' He suddenly released her and she rocked back on her feet. 'He didn't hang around for long, though. Or perhaps he came back tonight?'

'You stayed to spy on me?' Her eyes widened in surprise. Then a flash of anger sparked through them. 'You should have stayed longer, then you'd know whether he came back.'

'No!' He stepped back. 'No. I didn't do that. I was too angry to trust myself at the wheel of a car. I sat in the car park for a while, that's all, and I saw him leave, then a while later you all went back to the site.'

She frowned. 'I didn't notice the Aston in the car park.'

He shook his head. 'It needed some work. I borrowed a car from the garage. Look, Jo, this is silly. Can't we go inside and talk?'

She hesitated for a moment then shrugged and unlocked the door. 'Why not? I know I'll be safe in your company.' She threw her bag on the sofa and turned to face him. 'Won't I?'

3

'Maybe.' He seemed to fill her sitting-room. 'Have you eaten?'

'I'm not hungry, Clay. I'm just tired. All I want is a shower and my bed. Just say whatever it is you feel you have to and go.'

'You have to eat.' He turned her in the direction of the bedroom and firmly steered her towards it. 'Have your shower. I'll get you some food.'

She dug her heels in. 'I don't want anything from you, Clay.'

'Yes, you do.' His hands were still on her shoulders and his grip intensified. 'So you'd better go and shower now, before I lose all semblance of self-control and remind you exactly what you want from me.'

She fled. Locking the bathroom door firmly behind her, she stood against it, her whole body trembling with the longing for him to slake the shattering need that the slightest touch of hand awoke in her. A longing that wouldn't go away.

'Damn you, Clay Thackeray,' she whispered to herself. She took deep, calming breaths and gradually began to regain control of herself. Slowly she undressed, and stood under a fierce shower trying to work out what Clay wanted from her. She had already offered him everything a girl could give a man and he had rejected it in very short order. Angrily she flicked the switch to cold.

Shivering, she quickly dressed in cream cord trousers and an oversized fleecy sweatshirt. The blue was faded and the Prince of Wales feathers of Surrey Cricket Club were barely visible, but it had been her father's and it was a comfort in her misery.

As she opened the bedroom door she heard a key in the lock. Clay appeared carrying a plastic bag. 'I borrowed your key. Hope you don't mind.'

'When you said you were getting food, I had assumed you were going to cook,' she protested. 'I could have made an omelette or something.'

'You said you were tired,' he said. 'Have you got any chopsticks?'

'I'm afraid not. I just use knives and forks.' Her lips imitated a smile.

He shook his head and tutted. 'How very conventional.'

'I've recently discovered that stepping outside the bounds of convention isn't that good for my ego,' she replied, sharply.

He smiled. 'I promise I'll do my best to restore it.' With a wry smile he dumped a pile of magazines on the floor. '*New Civil Engineer*. I might as well be at home.'

'I'm sure I can find you a copy of *Vogue* if it will make you feel more comfortable,' she offered, but he ignored this and began to lay out a series of aluminum dishes on the glass-topped coffee-table.

'Plates?' he suggested.

'Has anyone ever told you that you have a very managing disposition, Clay Thackeray?' she remarked, crossly.

'Managing is what I do best, Joanna Grant, so you'd better get used to it.'

'Yes, sir,' Jo snapped, but fetched a couple of plates and some cutlery from the kitchen. Clay piled a plate with food and handed it to her. She stared at it in dismay. 'I can't eat all this!'

He helped himself to food. 'Convince me that you've had a proper meal today and I'll let you off with half,' he offered.

'I don't suppose you'd take a doughnut into consideration?' He paused in the act of spooning rice on to his plate just long enough to hand her a fork. She made no further protest. At least eating precluded conversation.

'More?' he offered, as he watched her finish.

Jo shook her head. 'No. But thank you.' She forced a smile. 'I was hungrier than I thought.' She began to clear the dishes into the kitchen. 'Now, perhaps you'll tell me why you're here?' It seemed easier to ask the question while she was occupied. 'What exactly do you want from me?'

He had followed her, and his voice at her ear made her jump 'Maybe,' he said, very softly, 'I did change my mind. Maybe I can't get the thought of the other night out of my head.' He reached out and caught her wrist. 'Maybe I've been driven to distraction by the thought of you offering yourself to another man . . . I have the feeling that Peter Lloyd wouldn't be so tactless as to refuse you. Or is that where you've been all weekend?'

Jo stared at his hand, at the strong fingers curled around her wrist, the same fingers that had elicited such a eager response from her. She ignored his question. 'Is that how you see me?' she asked. 'Desperate? Realising how late I've left it and throwing myself at every man who comes my way in the hope that one of them will take pity on me?' She shuddered, resisting to no purpose as he pulled her into his arms, wrapping them around her, holding her close.

'Is that how you see yourself?' She looked up into his eyes but, startled by the intensity of his expression, she buried her face in his sweater. 'Joanna?'

'It wasn't like that. I just never met anyone before . . . ' Her voice was muffled and he caught her shoulders and held her away from him.

'What wasn't it like?'

She concentrated very hard on the stocking-stitch pattern of his sweater. 'You were the first man I've met who just took my breath away. That's all.' The first to make her body sing, her heart do somersaults, her skin tingle. All the ridiculous things that people wrote in love songs.

'It's that simple?' he asked softly.

'Yes, it's that simple,' she lied. Love was never that simple. She raised long dark lashes and met his eyes head-on. 'You were right in a way, when you suggested that it had become a burden. Although I hadn't realised it myself.'

She gave a small sigh. 'It must be so much simpler if you fall head over heels in love when you're sixteen and get the sex thing over with.' She half smiled at herself. 'The older you get, Clay, the harder it becomes. You become choosier, it assumes an importance quite out of proportion to its significance. Then along comes a man who meets all the specifications.' She withdrew from his arms. He made a move to hold her but she put up her hand to keep him at bay. 'Someone experienced enough to make it special.' She dropped her hands to her sides and shrugged. 'I'm sorry to have complicated what to you must have seemed something very straightforward.'

'But you must have met dozens of men.' He sounded genuinely astonished.

'Hundreds,' she corrected him and smiled. 'My friends were convinced that I chose an engineering course because of the men. But the truth was that at university I was working far too hard to

70

get that involved. There was too much to prove.'

'And afterwards? Was there still too much to prove?'

'You mustn't flirt on site, Clay. Not if you expect to be taken seriously. And you get moved about. It's not that easy.'

'It seemed very easy . . . ' He stopped as she swung away from him, walking swiftly into the living-room, leaning her cheek against the cool glass and staring sightlessly out of the window. 'I'm sorry, Jo. That came out all wrong. But it was easy, don't you see? It wasn't just you. I wanted to carry you off to bed the moment I set eyes on you.' He chuckled softly. 'It was quite a relief to find out that you were a girl, I can tell you.' He came up behind her and put his arms around her and rubbed his cheeks against her hair. 'The chemistry was right.'

'Chemistry?' she asked a little breathlessly, as she felt his body stir against her and the instant liquid fire course through her veins as he dragged her back against him.

'Lust at first sight.' His voice grated softly at her ear. 'So we'd better do something about it, don't you think?'

Lust? Surely it had been more than that, even for him? 'Desire' was the word that sprang unbidden to her mind. Or was that merely a euphemism for the raw need he had so unexpectedly awoken in her? Burning her from the inside out so that she thought she might explode if he didn't assuage her longing with his lips, his hands . . . She shuddered. Whatever it was he was offering, she wanted him.

'Now?' she asked.

'Such flattering impatience, my love. But there are one or two details to be sorted out first. Friday's a good day for me. And we'll have known one another for two weeks. That's almost respectable.'

She gasped, turning sharply in the circle of his arms to face him. For the second time she had offered him everything she had to give, and this time he had to consult his diary?

'A whole day, my love?' She echoed his endearment coldly. 'Are you sure you can spare it?'

His voice was cool. 'I think I can spare a whole day for our wedding.'

'Wedding?' She was sure she had misheard him.

'Well? Do you accept my proposal?'

'What proposal?'

'Just this. If you want my body you're going to have to take it on a permanent basis. Marry me, Joanna Grant.'

'That wasn't a proposal, Clay, it was a command.'

His mouth described a curve from her ear, along the line of her jaw, and for a moment she clung to him, the heady sensation of his lips against her skin driving the ability to reason from her mind.

'Do you prefer that?'

'I hardly know you,' she objected, faintly.

'You hardly knew me on Friday,' he pointed out, with perfect accuracy. 'It didn't seem to matter then.'

She blushed furiously. 'That was different.'

'No, it wasn't.' He wrapped his arms about her, regarding her upturned face from under heavy lids. 'Not a bit different.' Before she could extricate herself, his hands were sliding under her sweatshirt and stroking the satin skin of her naked back. His brows shot up. 'No underwear, Miss Grant? How very shocking.' His hands moved to caress her throbbing breasts, his thumbs brushing the hard budding tips. Then his mouth was on hers and his kiss was binding her to him with the fierce promise of untasted pleasures.

When at last he raised his head, she clung to him weakly. 'I don't know what to say.'

'There's nothing to say, my darling. You've already answered me.'

She took a slow, deep breath and shook her head. 'You don't have to marry me, Clay.'

'I believe you made that plain

enough.' A telltale muscle was working at the corner of his mouth. 'But I'm making it a condition.'

'Why, Clay? People don't marry for *lust*.'

'Really? Why else would they marry?' He held her lightly, felt her betraying body tremble in his arms and, certain now of victory, he smiled. 'I want you, Jo. And when I saw you kiss Lloyd today I knew just how badly I wanted you.'

'That's silly . . . ' she protested.

'Is it?' His voice was silky. 'Convince me.' When he finally lifted his head his breathing was as ragged as hers, his eyes almost black with naked hunger. For a moment he held her so fiercely that she thought he would never release her. Then he drew in a great shuddering breath. 'Friday?' he demanded harshly.

She nodded dumbly, quite unable to speak.

'Witch,' he murmured. 'If you knew more, you would be positively danger-ous.' He stroked her cheek with the edge of his thumb. 'I'll pick you up in the morning. We can choose a ring. Nine-thirty. Don't be late.'

★   ★   ★

It had been an odd week. She had telephoned her office to ask if she could have the rest of the week as part of her leave, but had told no one why she wanted the time off. She had always kept her work completely separate from her private life and saw no reason to change simply because she was getting married.

Her family had been another matter altogether. But Jo had weathered the storm of her mother's disapproval at such a rushed marriage.

'It's madness, Jo!' Her mother had never called her Joanna, she reflected absently. Her father always had, and her sister sometimes, but never her mother. 'What about your career, your ambitions?' she said angrily after Clay had called formally to meet her. 'I guarantee that he'll have you pregnant on your honeymoon and you might as well never have gone to university.'

'Leave her alone, Mum.' Her sister grinned knowingly. 'Not that I disagree in general with your conclusions. Would you like me to help you choose your outfit?' she offered.

Jo accepted with grateful thanks. Heather, ten years her senior and a fashion buyer before the twins had arrived, and she'd begun to run her own boutique, had exquisite taste. She had already turned over the stock at a bridal wear store and picked out three outfits for Jo to try on when she arrived somewhat breathlessly on Wednesday morning.

'Perfect, love,' Heather pronounced, when Jo decided on a simple ivory suit in wild silk. 'Not many women can wear a straight skirt, but you have such a narrow waist and a perfectly beautiful little bottom . . . ' She laughed as Jo blushed. 'He's already told you that.' She gently lifted the wide shawl collar to frame Jo's face. 'This collar is beautiful. It's a good thing you're a standard size; you haven't allowed yourself much time. Although I don't think you could have done better than that in three years, let alone three days.' She laughed. 'And I'm not sure I'm talking about the clothes. Are you going to wear a hat? Try this one.' Obediently Jo tried on the tiny pillbox and immediately took it off again.

'I don't think so. I don't think I've got the right shape head for a hat.'

Heather giggled. 'Not that one, anyway. This might be more you. No, close your eyes.' She fastened the circle of stiffened silk to Jo's head. 'Now look,' she said, with satisfaction.

Jo opened her eyes and for a moment stared at the stranger reflected in the mirror.

'Not bad, eh?' Heather beamed. 'Been hiding your light under Dad's old Barbour for too long. Clay's a clever man to spot you.'

'I took the Barbour off, Heather.'

'I think you'd better stop there, or I might just get jealous. Has he told you where he's taking you for your honeymoon?'

'We only have the weekend. He's in the middle of some business deal.'

'It must be something big to put your honeymoon on hold?'

'Very big.' Jo's smile was automatic. The truth was, she had no idea what the deal was.

★   ★   ★

'You look utterly charming, my dear.' Clay's father kissed her cheek. 'I'm so glad you didn't make him wait too long.'

'I . . . he was very insistent,' Jo said and blushed.

'Was he?' The older man regarded his son with affection. 'No point in fighting it, then. He always did get anything he set his mind on. I remember when — '

'I think we can do without nursery tales, if you don't mind.' Clay took Jo's hand and led her firmly away from the small group of family and friends who had come to witness the wedding. 'There hasn't been a moment to tell you how very beautiful you look.' He glanced at their guests and bent his head to her ear. 'Is there any way we could miss lunch, do you think?'

'Such flattering impatience,' she teased him. 'And you're the one who insisted on waiting.'

'Right now I can't think why.'

But eventually lunch was over, the cake had been cut and they had extricated themselves from their well-wishers. Clay drove the Aston through the country roads, turning at last into the lane that led to the river and his cottage. He pulled into the driveway and turned off the engine and silence descended around them.

'Welcome home, Mrs Thackeray.'

'Would you mind very much if I continue to call myself Grant?' she asked, as he took her hand and helped her from the car.

His fingers tightened around hers. 'You want to keep your own name?' His brows drew together as he frowned. 'You have some objection to mine?'

'None whatever, Clay. It's a splendid name. It's just simpler for work.' She lowered her lashes. 'Besides, I married you for your body, not your name.' Then she blushed crimson.

He touched her cheek with his fingers. 'So you did,' he said thoughtfully, then with a shrug he took her arm in his and they walked arm in arm down the path. Clay unlocked the door then turned to her, the slightest smile playing about his lips. 'Shall I carry you over the threshold, *Miss Grant*, or do your unexpectedly feminist views preclude that?'

'Why should they do that?' she asked, a sudden *frisson* of nerves catching in her voice as she noted the dangerous gleam lighting his eyes.

'Because carrying a bride over the threshold harks back to the caveman tactics of slinging the nearest breeding female over your shoulder and carrying her off to mate.'

She laughed a little uncertainly. 'Perhaps we should both step over the threshold together to signify our complete equality — '

'Rubbish!' He didn't wait for her to finish, but picked her up and threw her effortlessly over his shoulder.

'Clay! Let me go!' she protested furiously. He didn't bother to answer, but pushed the front door closed behind him with his foot and carried her kicking and yelling up the stairs, while her hat and shoes flew in all directions.

'Mind the beam,' he cautioned, as he ducked, then he dumped her on the wide bed. She scrambled quickly to the far side as he joined her and jumped to her feet.

'Clay, I won't — ' she said, backing away as he advanced towards her.

'Won't what, Miss Grant?' he breathed. And then she was trapped, cornered and he was towering over her. 'Don't you want your wedding present?'

Her mouth dried. She hadn't expected him to be like this. All week he had been so careful not to push the fine strands of self-restraint to breaking-point. Now something seemed to have snapped. She gave a little scream as he caught her wrist and turned it over, raising it to his lips to kiss the delicate blue-veined skin, crossing the palm of her hand with butterfly touches of his lips, teasing the tips of her fingers. He raised his eyes, and she saw then that it was a game and he was laughing.

'Beast!' she said, but softly.

'Not today,' he promised. 'Not yet.'

She discovered that her legs were trembling and as she put out her hands to save herself he caught her and pulled her into his arms.

'And I really do have a present for you.' He took a small box from his pocket and opened it. Inside nestled a small gold Victorian locket. 'It was my mother's.'

'Clay, it's beautiful. Will you put it on for me?' He lifted the locket from the box and she turned and bent her head so that he could fasten it. His fingers brushed teasingly against her neck and she heard a small noise that might have come from somewhere inside her. He caught her hair, raking it away from her neck with his fingers.

'Do you know,' he murmured, 'that in Japan a geisha leaves the nape of her neck unpainted because it is considered to be exquisitely erotic?' He explored the delicate, sensitive skin with his lips, with the tip of his tongue, until she was gasping, breathless as a wave of desire swept over her.

'What else do geishas do?' Jo's voice was husky as he turned her to face him.

His lids drooped lazily, hooding the dazzling blue. 'Why don't you use your imagination?'

'But I don't know — '

'You wanted my body, darling. Take it. It's all yours.'

A tremor contracted her abdomen and her breathing shortened as she reached up to smooth the jacket away from his shoulders. She stretched it carefully across the back of a chair, certain that no self-respecting geisha would drop it on the floor. Then she loosened his tie, taking care not to touch him more than necessary, sliding the silk free of the knot. She folded it and laid it neatly on the chair. Her fingers began to shake as she undid the buttons of his shirt. She glanced up and saw that Clay was holding himself rigid as she slipped each tiny disc from its fastening and she smiled, deep down inside where he couldn't see.

At last it was done. She loosened the shirt, pulling it from his trousers, gently resting her cheek against his chest as she reached behind to free the back. His heart was beating as fast as her own and she brought her hands back to the front, fluttering her fingertips against his skin, over the little whorls of hair, across the small male nipples.

He groaned then and captured her, crushing her against him, his mouth hard on hers. She revelled in the sweet, heady sensation of her victory over his self-control. When, finally, he pulled away for lack of breath, she smiled.

'Shall I go on now?' she asked, but he captured her hands.

'I believe it's my turn.' He undid the three large buttons that fastened her jacket and pushed it back from her shoulders, leaving it to drop to the floor as his hands lingered to trace the long column of her neck. He stroked her gently, the backs of his fingers following her breastbone until they came to rest on her proud cleavage. He bent swiftly and buried his face there and with a cry she caught his head and held him, her fingers twisting in the thick dark curls. There was a sudden welcome freedom from the irksome restraint of lace, then with a fierce shout he lifted her and carried her bodily to the bed.

★   ★   ★

Joanna turned and woke to find Clay lying on his side watching her.

'If you were a cat, Joanna, you would be purring,' he said, at last.

'If I were a cat, my love, you would be stroking me.' She stretched in invitation and he laughed softly as she turned into his arms. Three nights and two days had only increased the first ecstatic pleasure of their lovemaking, but now, as she curved against him, he seized her and held her away.

'No, you don't. Honeymoon's over, my sweet. I have to work today, God help me.'

'Work?' She let the word sink in. Then sat up with a shock. 'Clay, it's Monday!'

'Yes,' he said, wryly. 'It's Monday.'

'What time is it?'

'Seven o'clock. But there's no need for you to get up.'

She scrambled from the bed. 'I'll be late.'

'Late?' He sat up, his hands clasped behind his head, watching her scrambling through the drawers. 'Where are you going? Arranged some shopping trip with the delectable Heather?'

'Don't be silly, Clay. I'm going to work.' She found a pair of jeans and held them up. 'Are these mine, or yours?' She turned and suddenly realised that he was very still. 'What's the matter?'

'I just hadn't realised that you intended to rush back to work. I thought you might spend a few more days totally dedicated to my well-being.'

'Stay at home with me and I'll consider it.' Her generous mouth curved in a smile as she dropped the trousers, and moved towards him.

He caught her wrist before she could wreak havoc on his will. 'I'm sorry, Jo. I did warn you — '

'It must be something very special,' she said, hoping that he might elaborate.

'I'll be back as soon as I can.' He pulled her down and kissed her. 'I promise. Sure you won't stay and keep the bed warm?'

'That's not much of a career move.'

'Isn't it? I thought you might find me a full-time job.'

She straightened. 'Why would you think that, Clay?'

'I can't imagine. Fantasising, no doubt.'

'I'm not the domestic type. Even as a little girl I was always better at mud pies than pastry. What on earth would I do about the house all day?'

He rose in one smooth movement and was at her side. 'I had this vision of you, my darling, in a frilly apron, dusting the bedrooms, baking apple pie — '

Her eyes widened in horror. 'You didn't!'

His face split into a grin. 'No, that wasn't exactly the role I had in mind. Mrs Johnson already does that to perfection.' Jo had met the lady who kept the cottage immaculate and had taken great pains to reassure her that she had no intention of usurping her role. Clay looked suddenly serious. 'But the kitchen garden could do with a good weeding.'

'Sorry. I can't tell a weed from an orchid.'

'It's easy, darling. If you pull it up and it grows again it was a weed. If you pull it up — '

' — and it doesn't grow again, it was the orchid,' she finished.

'Ah, well. It was a nice try. But being married to a career-woman will take a bit of getting used to.' He kissed her shoulder and she turned, dropping the jeans as she reached for him, but he held her at bay. 'It's as well that I have an early meeting, or you, Miss Grant, would be very late for work. Very late indeed.' He kissed her hard then turned her firmly in the direction of the bathroom. 'Don't be long.'

They made an odd pair at breakfast, Clay all tailored elegance in a dark suit and a striped shirt, Joanna in denims and a jumper that had seen better days.

'What time will you be home?'

Joanna added an apple to her lunch-box and considered the question. 'I have to finish clearing the flat.

There's not too much left there so I suppose I could do it at lunchtime. But we need some shopping; the fridge is pretty bare.'

'You'll want some money.' He took a wallet out of his inside pocket and offered her some notes. 'Take this for now. I'll organise a housekeeping account for you.'

'I don't need that, Clay. We'll have to sort out some sort of split on expenses.' His expression didn't change and yet she had the feeling she had said something to make him angry. 'The mortgage and so on,' she added, uncertainly, realising as she said the words that she hadn't a clue if there was, in fact, a mortgage on the cottage, or anything very much about Clay Thackeray except that she loved him beyond all reason. But she didn't want him to think that she had married him for a free ride.

A smile creased his eyes and it was all right. 'Thanks for the offer, Jo. But I think I can manage to support us both in reasonable comfort. Besides, you won't always be a working girl, will you? Once the babies begin to arrive you won't be able to contribute to the — er — mortgage.'

'Babies?' She felt a tiny stab of unease.

'You do know where they come from?' he teased. 'Or haven't you been paying attention . . . ?'

'Yes.' Her voice sounded unnaturally loud and she forced her mouth into an answering curve. 'I just hadn't realised it was the gooseberry bushes that needed weeding.'

'I'd better get someone in to do it.' He dropped the notes on the table and stood up. 'I'll be home around seven. Do you want Mrs Johnson to leave something, or will you prefer to cook?'

'I'll cook,' Jo said, without thinking.

'Whatever you like.' He glanced at his watch. 'I've got to go.' He took her in his arms and kissed her with a sweet, fierce urgency that quite took her breath away. 'Take care.'

Jo drove to work but when she arrived couldn't remember any of the ten miles she had negotiated. Once the babies arrived? Her mother had suggested he would want a family immediately, but she had dismissed the idea as ridiculous. Men didn't want families. Babies were things that women yearned for and men put up with as the price for a home, food on the table, a willing partner in bed. She worked with men all day. She heard the things they said, knew what they got up to in the lunch-hours when their wives were worn out with housework and children. Even Heather's husband had briefly strayed when she had been huge with the twins — She cut off the thought. It didn't matter. It wouldn't ever happen to her.

She sighed and reluctantly let the warm memory of Clay's lovemaking go, firmly banishing thoughts of him as far to the back of her mind as he was prepared to stay. She was a career-woman, she reminded herself, but keeping her personal life separate from work had been easier when she hadn't had a personal life.

She spent the morning immersed in the problems that no one else had bothered with during her absence, glad enough, at lunchtime, of a genuine excuse to refuse Peter Lloyd's flirtatious offer of a drink.

'I'm moving the last of my things from the flat,' she said, without thinking.

'You're moving?' he asked, with unexpected interest.

'Yes. Excuse me, I don't have much time.'

'You'll have to let Personnel know your new address. And I'll want your telephone number.' It was a perfectly reasonable request, yet, as always, he managed to endow the simplest request with some hidden meaning.

'My number hasn't changed. I have a portable phone.' She certainly wasn't giving him the cottage number. Cursing herself silently for being so careless, she hurried away before he could ask any more questions. The less he knew about her life, the better.

4

Married life, Jo decided happily, was a lot more fun than living on your own. Waking up to find the man you loved smiling at you was the very best way to start the day. Especially when he then proceeded to kiss her.

'I'm working from home today,' he murmured, throatily, pulling her close. 'Don't rush away.'

The temptation to linger in his arms was almost too much, but today was special and she had to be strong.

'Sorry, my love. You chose the wrong day.' She laughed and tried to wriggle free, but he held her without apparent effort. 'Please, Clay,' she begged as his lips teased her throat. 'I have a meeting at eight o'clock. I want to make a good impression.'

His eyes darkened and for a moment his hands tightened around her waist.

Then he released her and rolled on to his back. 'In that case, sweetheart, it would be cruel to detain you,' he said, carelessly. 'Although in my day site engineers weren't invited to meetings.'

'The senior engineer has left, so I'm standing in for him.' It was essential that he understand how important it was to her. 'I'm going to apply for his job. I've as good a chance as anyone. I must make a good impression.' He made no response, and if it hadn't been so silly she could have sworn that he was angry. 'Clay?' She smiled uncertainly. 'I can't be late.'

There was no answering smile. 'If it's so important to you, you'd better get a move on.'

'Don't make me choose, Clay.'

He turned to her, his face unreadable. 'Would it be so very difficult?'

She didn't bother to make breakfast. Instead she slammed the door hard on her way out and drove to work through a film of tears, angry with him for not understanding, even angrier with herself, although she didn't know why.

The meeting seemed endless; Jo's mind kept wandering to Clay, wondering what he was doing. But at last it was over and someone moved that they adjourn to the pub for an early lunch.

'Coming, Jo?' Peter's proprietorial hand was at her back as they stood outside the site office.

She had acquitted herself well at the meeting despite the mental distraction and relief made her generous with her smile. 'You've all held yourselves in check on my account for quite long enough,' she said, excusing herself. She patted Peter's cheek lightly and extricated herself from his grasp. 'You'll enjoy your lunch much more if you don't have to think twice before you tell a joke.' And she could spend the time far more usefully going home to make her peace with Clay. But she didn't have to go home, because as she turned away she saw him.

Clay, clad in close-fitting jeans and a

white shirt that billowed loosely, giving him something of the appearance of seventeenth-century pirate, was leaning against the Aston, arms folded, watching them with an ominous intensity. Her heart in her boots, she detached herself from the group and went over to him.

'Hello, Clay,' she said, stiff, in the face of his all too evident displeasure. 'How lovely to see you.'

'Is it?' He opened the car door and held it for her, his eyes daring her to do anything other than get in. She slid into the seat but he didn't speak again until he pulled into a quiet turning and parked under some trees. She turned on him.

'Well? What do you want?'

He stared straight ahead, through the windscreen, his knuckles white where he gripped the wheel. 'I'm not quite sure. I know that I came to apologise for this morning. I wanted you to stay with me. Understandable, but not exactly fair.'

'No. Not exactly fair.' She glanced at him uncertainly. He sounded reasonable enough, but she wasn't convinced. 'If one of the men had been late, you see, no one would have said a word. But I have to be . . . well, I don't have to spell it out, do I?'

He ignored this. 'But then I came face to face with my wife, my very professional wife, a wife who is so very professional that she prefers people to think she isn't married, and who mustn't be late for meetings on any account, flirting with that pompous ass.'

'Tell me, Clay,' she said, making her voice very quiet, in her determination not to shout, 'what do you object to most? The flirting? Or the fact that I chose to do it with a pompous ass?'

'Both!' He seized her shoulders and glared angrily at her for a moment. 'If I see that man lay so much as a finger on you again, I'll knock that expensive dentistry clean down his throat. And — '

'And what?' she demanded. 'What

will you do to me, Clay? Shake me like a naughty schoolgirl, until my teeth rattle?'

For a moment he held her, his fingers biting painfully into her shoulders. Then, with effort, he slowly regained possession of himself.

'There would be little point in that. I'm perfectly aware that you can't be browbeaten by me, or anyone else. But I do have one weapon that we both know you can't resist.'

Rigid with anger at his distrust, she told herself that right now resistance would be easy. But his mouth on hers was warm, gentle, and as his hands slid from her shoulders to her back, drawing her closer, she whimpered, quite unable to help herself.

When, apparently satisfied that he had proved his point, he at last let her go, she blinked back a film of tears, feeling totally humiliated by the casual ease with which he could dominate her body.

'I should have done that this

morning,' he said angrily.

'My job is important to me, Clay.'

He grasped her chin and forced her to face him.

'You've made that abundantly clear. If you want to be a career-woman, Jo, you've got it. And you can call yourself Miss Grant until the cows come home if it pleases you. But don't ever forget you're my wife. First, last and everything in between.'

'Why should I want to forget?' she demanded through angry tears. 'Why on earth do you think I married you?'

The curve of his mouth was pure insolence. 'You married me, Joanna, because your body suddenly realised what it was made for. And because I wanted you to.'

'Did you? Why? Just why *did* you marry me?' she demanded.

For a moment he stared at her. Then he turned abruptly away and he reached for the ignition. 'I'll take you back.'

He dropped her off just as the others

came back from the pub and they stood watching the car with open admiration as it disappeared down the road. Peter Lloyd stopped her as she passed him. 'Who was that?'

She didn't want to talk to him, would give anything never to set eyes on him again. 'Clay Thackeray,' she answered as briefly as she could.

'Thackeray,' he repeated thoughtfully. 'Clay Thackeray. The name rings a bell. What does he do?'

'Do?' she asked, coldly.

'It's probably just a coincidence, but I saw him at the office yesterday being given the grand tour. There have been all sorts of rumours flying around about a take-over ever since Charles Redmond's heart attack. The company has a big fat pension fund. Very tempting for a certain type of businessman.'

'What sort?' she asked, curious despite herself.

'The sort that only cares for profit and doesn't give a damn about the little people who make it for him.'

'Clay isn't like that,' she said, shocked. 'He's a civil engineer. He knew my father.'

He gave her a long, hard look. 'Well, you probably know far more about it than me; you've that nice parcel of shares your father left you. But better beware.' He leered suggestively. 'Mr Thackeray might just have more than one motive for romancing you.'

'I'm sorry, I've heard nothing. Will you excuse me, please?' She didn't wait for his reply. But in the privacy of the office she searched in her handbag for the letter she had received from the solicitors with an increased offer for her shares.

He had seemed to know. And his arrival had coincided with her rejection of the first offer. For a long time she stared at it. Then, her heart hammering painfully in her throat, she reached for the telephone. It had been stupid to ignore it. If she knew nothing about an attempted take-over she had no one but herself to blame. She had a responsibility to Redmonds and to herself as a shareholder. The least she could do was find out what was going on. Not that she thought Clay was involved, not for one moment. But, when she had asked him why he had married her, he hadn't given her an answer. And he hadn't mentioned his visit to Redmonds.

The simple truth was that she hardly knew more about his business activities now than on the day they met. On their marriage licence he had stated his occupation as company director. When she had asked him what company he had smiled.

'Half a dozen at the last count, but it's all right, I don't expect you to have heard of any of them.' Then he had kissed her, his warm mouth driving all other thoughts from her mind.

That evening she pulled an old shoe-box out of her wardrobe and found her share certificate. It was worth more than money to her. Her father had helped Charles Redmond when the company hit a bad patch years earlier. He had borrowed on his life assurance and this block of shares had been his reward. Redmond had wanted him to join the board, but her father had declined. He wasn't interested in the wheeling and dealing of company finance. He had been a civil engineer and never wanted to be anything else. And he had left the shares to her because in a man's world she would need an 'edge'. She hadn't expected them to come to her so soon and had felt, guiltily, that her mother should have had them. But her mother had taken her father's view and refused her offer.

'What are you doing?' Startled, Jo looked up from the floor, where she was sitting surrounded by papers. She hadn't heard him come up the stairs.

'I was looking for something.' She tried to push the certificate back into its folder, but Clay stopped alongside her and took it from her hands. He examined it thoughtfully then met her watchful eyes.

'This should be in the safe downstairs, Jo,' he said. 'It's a very valuable document.'

'I know.' His eyebrows rose sharply at the abruptness of her reply. 'I thought it should be in the bank,' she hedged. 'That's why I was looking for it.'

'Have you decided to sell them after all?' There was a more than casual interest, she thought, although his expression was carefully shuttered. She tried to remember whether she had mentioned that the offer had been for Redmonds' shares. She thought not.

'I have no plans to sell them at the moment. I just thought the certificate should be kept more securely.'

'You're right. Would you like me to do it for you? It could just as easily be kept in my safety deposit box.' She wondered, uneasily, if simply possessing the certificate so that she would be unable to sell to anyone else would be enough, the 'edge' that he might need if he was trying to gain control of Redmonds.

'I . . . The arrangements have already been made. I'm going up to town tomorrow.'

'I see.' He surrendered it to her, unwillingly, she thought. 'In that case I'll leave it for you to deal with. Look after it.'

She placed it back in its folder and attempted to gather the rest of the papers together, but his brooding presence made her clumsy. Finally he swept them up and shuffled them up into some order before handing them back to her. They had hardly spoken beyond the need for politeness since she had come home. Now he touched her cheek very gently.

'It's a lovely evening, Jo. Why don't we take a walk along the towpath?'

She made an effort at a smile. 'A walk?'

'Just as far as the Ferry? For a drink?'

'Yes, if you like. I'll be right with you.'

The river was busy. A fine July had brought out the pleasure boats, and the holiday cruisers were already thick on the water. For a while they walked without speaking. Jo couldn't think what to say that wouldn't bring them back to the reason for the strained atmosphere. Then Clay spotted a family of ducks and caught her hand as he pointed to them.

'There's a nest just by our mooring,' Jo said, her voice shaking with the helpless longing to forget everything that had happened since she got up this morning and go back to yesterday. 'They haven't hatched yet . . . ' Her voice trailed away.

They walked on. 'I've been meaning to talk to you about the mooring. Have you any strong feelings about boats?'

'In what way?'

'Any way.'

'No,' she said. 'I don't think so. But then I've never been in anything bigger than a dinghy with an outboard motor.'

'I can do a little better than that. I had someone over this morning to look at the boathouse. I've decided to have it restored.'

'Restored?' She considered the possibility of restoring the collapsed heap that glorified in the name of boathouse. 'There's precious little left to restore. Surely a more appropriate word would be 'rebuilt'?'

'Perhaps.' He almost smiled. 'But rebuilt to the original plan. I should have saved myself the fee and consulted you.'

'I should have thought you could have worked that out for yourself.'

'I could do it all myself, Jo, from the foundations up. But it wouldn't be a cost-effective use of my time.'

'Wouldn't it?' She tried not to dwell on exactly what he considered an appropriate use of his time.

'Well, I'd need a labourer. How would you feel about taking the job on?'

'It might be fun,' she said, her mind smiling at the thought of the two of them working together. Reluctantly she switched the picture off. 'But I take your point. Who is going to do the work?'

'Redmonds. They do a lot of work on the river so they were the obvious choice.'

'Redmonds! Oh, that's wonderful.' The words were expelled on a sudden breath of relief at such a simple explanation for his presence in the office. She had been screwing herself up to ask him about it. Now suddenly it was all right.

'I'm glad you're so pleased,' he said drily. 'I thought I'd better keep it in the family.' He had stopped and was looking at her oddly. 'What is it?'

'Absolutely nothing.' She threw her arms around his neck. She knew she was grinning idiotically, but couldn't help herself. 'Except I'm incredibly hungry.'

'Are you?' His arms were around her waist, drawing her against him. 'Well, you had no lunch and you didn't eat much dinner.'

'Neither did you. Perhaps I should leave the cooking to Mrs Johnson.'

'There's nothing wrong with your cooking. I just didn't feel like . . . ' He stopped. 'Jo, let's go home.'

Later, lying in the darkness, Jo went

through the day again in her mind, trying to work out why it had gone so dreadfully wrong. It all came down to trust, she decided. Clay had no reason to be jealous of Peter, stupidly over-reacting to what he imagined he had seen. And she had been no better. The slightest hint that Clay might be working against the best interests of Redmonds and its staff had raised her suspicions. Because, she decided, sleep-ily, outside of bed she and Clay were still relative strangers. But that was something time would mend. She smiled as he drew her into the circle of his arms.

'Go to sleep,' he murmured.

'Make me.'

* * *

'If you're coming up to town today,' Clay said, over breakfast, 'why don't you come to the office?' Jo jumped guiltily. How on earth had Clay found out that she was going to the solicitors today? 'You did say you were taking your share certificate to the bank.' His expression was appraising and she knew her cheeks had gone a betraying shade of pink. 'Unless of course you have some other plans?'

'Oh, no.' And even as she said the words she knew she should have told him. But it was too late. She made an effort to pull herself together. 'That is, I'd love to see your office. I'll be finished by twelve, I should think.'

'In that case I'll have my secretary write in 'Miss Grant' for lunch.' He stood up and dropped a kiss on the top of her head. 'Don't be late.'

'No, sir! See you later.'

At eleven o'clock she was in the city office of a firm of solicitors that appeared to have been in business since Victoria came to the throne. It was possible, she thought, that one or two of the staff were the original employees.

But Mr Henry Doubleday was not one of them. Smooth, well groomed, he put himself out to charm her. Yet when she rose half an hour later she was hardly any wiser. She had an offer for her shares from a gentleman who preferred to remain anonymous. An offer that Mr Doubleday took great pains to point out was well above the market value.

She asked if anyone else had been approached, but he 'wasn't at liberty to say'. She asked why the gentleman was prepared to pay so much. That, again, was confidential. She asked how they knew she had the shares and he told her that it was a matter of public record. She hadn't realised that.

It quickly became clear that she would learn nothing from this man. Not that it mattered any more. She excused herself, promising to give the offer further thought. She had intended to give some truth to her lie and go to the bank to leave the share certificate, but, glancing at her watch, she realised she would have to leave it until after lunch. She hailed a cab and gave the driver the address of Clay's office, which turned out to be an impressive city block.

The lift took her to the twenty-first floor and she stepped into an impressive, thickly carpeted foyer presided over by a beautiful red-headed receptionist. The girl ran an expert assessing eye over Jo's clothes and clearly found her suit wanting.

'Mr Thackeray is expecting me,' Jo said, interrupting the examination. 'Joanna Grant.'

'Miss Joanna Grant?' she asked, consulting her list. A second appraisal apparently confirmed her first opinion that this woman had no business bothering the likes of Clay Thackeray. Jo nodded and the girl waved at a chair with a sigh. 'Take a seat. I'll see if he's free.' The girl's offhand manner might have been amusing if Jo had felt less vulnerable, and for the first time she felt a pang of regret at retaining her own name. Then she dismissed the feeling as ridiculous. When she made it to the top of her profession everyone must know she was Joe Grant's daughter.

The girl telephoned and seconds later Clay was there, extending his hand in formal welcome. 'Miss Grant, how kind of you to come.' His expression was deadpan and she took the proffered hand and shook it gravely.

'Mr Thackeray? I've heard so much about you.'

'Should I be worried?' he asked, earnestly.

'Very!' she whispered. Then, louder, as she looked about her, 'I'm looking forward to seeing your offices.'

'I'm afraid there's no time now.' He placed a hand at her elbow and moved her firmly towards the lift, pausing briefly at the receptionist's desk. 'I should be back by two-thirty, but if Henry arrives before I do give him some coffee and tell him I won't keep him long.' His smile was warm.

'Yes, Clay.' The girl's eyes devoured him and Jo subdued with difficulty a wild stab of jealousy. The lift doors slid open. They stepped inside and she turned on him.

'Does that girl know you're married?'

'I'm not in the habit of discussing my private life with my staff. An attitude you should find some sympathy with.' His expression was unreadable. 'Does she bother you?'

'Should she?' She thought she was smiling. She hoped she was.

'Apparently she does.' He raised one shoulder in the slightest shrug, then smiled. 'I'll make you a promise, Jo. The day you agree to use the name Thackeray, I'll put an announcement in every national newspaper to tell the world that you're my wife.'

'I'll let you know,' she said, with a carelessness she was far from feeling.

'Any time.' The doorman hailed a cab and Clay told the man to take them to Greek Street and they were disgorged a while later at the restaurant door.

They were directed upstairs and shown to a table in the far corner. 'We'll be able to see everyone from here,' Clay said. Jo looked around her with interest at the signed photographs of actors and actresses that covered the pale green walls. Her eye halted on a familiar face at a nearby table.

'Isn't that — ?'

Clay didn't take his eyes off her. 'I expect so. It usually is whoever you think it is.'

They both ordered monkfish in a shellfish sauce and sat back to enjoy the comings and goings of the famous, and Jo forgot about shares and concrete and beautiful redheads as Clay set out to amuse her.

'Do you come here much?' she asked after the waiter had brought them a dish of strawberries. 'Everyone seems to know you.'

'Now and then. When I want to entertain special people.'

'Who, for instance?'

His eyes flickered over her and he smiled. 'Just business, Jo.'

She fiddled with her spoon. 'I don't think you ever told me exactly what your business is.'

'No.' He sat back, regarding her

thoughtfully. 'There always seems to be so many more interesting things to do when I'm with you.'

She blushed faintly. 'You could tell me now.'

His dark brows drew together. 'Is it important?'

'I'm interested in everything about you,' she said, and sipped her wine as her mouth dried.

He shrugged. 'I told you, I'm a consultant. I identify problems in the management structure of companies and put them right.'

'But you're a civil engineer,' she said, confused by this slightly ominous reply.

'Initially, yes. But, unlike your father, Joanna, I never found concrete to be an all-absorbing interest.'

'You would have taken the seat on the board,' she murmured, more to herself than him, but he immediately picked her up.

'Seat on the board?'

She found herself telling him about the time her father had helped Charles

Redmond save the company and his refusal to join the board.

'I hadn't realised that Joe had been offered a directorship. He should have taken it.' He regarded her thoughtfully. 'Maybe you should demand it now.'

Startled, she looked down to hide the sudden reawakening of all her fears from his all-seeing eyes.

'Don't be silly. I know nothing about business.'

'Nothing?' She held her breath momentarily, convinced that the time had come and he was going to ask her for her shares. Instead he laughed. 'If keeping your share certificates in a shoe-box is anything to go by, I would have to agree.'

She let out a long sigh of relief. 'It was Dad's box.'

'Do you know something? I'm not a bit surprised. If your father had hopped to work on one leg you would probably do the same.'

The fierceness in his voice shook her. 'I'm not . . . ' Her voice trailed away under his scornful look.

'Aren't you?'

She took a deep breath. 'I always wanted to be just like him, Clay. He was so funny. So clever. And when he took me to see the huge things that he had made I wanted to do it too.' More than that she would not say.

He took her hand. 'Joe Grant was one of the best men I've ever met, my love, but I never wanted to marry him, even at one remove. And he had his faults like everyone else. Perhaps it's time you tried being Joanna. She has a right to a life of her own.'

His perception was frightening. She turned quickly away and, spotting a new celebrity, diverted his attention and the moment passed.

It was only when she was on the train and the ticket collector asked to see her ticket that she realised she still had the share certificate in her bag.

It had been an inconclusive day, she thought, unhappily. She had found out nothing that was any real help. If

Charles Redmond had been available she would have gone to see him. But he was recuperating in the south of France from a mild heart attack and wouldn't be back for another couple of weeks.

It occurred to her that he might not even know what was going on, and she pondered on the wisdom of writing to him. She didn't want to give him another heart attack. But there was no reason why she couldn't write to ask how he was, just mentioning the offer casually, asking his advice. And, the decision made, she felt instantly better. She didn't know why she hadn't thought of that sooner. Instead of going back to the site, she called at the office to get his address from his secretary.

She was sitting at her dressing-table sealing the envelope when she heard Clay calling.

'Jo? Where are you? I've got something to tell you.' His feet pounded up the stairs and she jumped guiltily as the door swung open. As she turned her bag crashed to the floor, its contents sliding and rolling across the polished boards.

Clay surveyed the wreckage with amusement. 'Come on, I'll give you a hand.'

Jo's eyes fastened on the envelope containing the share certificate, convinced that Clay would be able to see straight through the thick manila.

'Leave it. I'll clear it up in a minute. What's your news?' She tried to distract him. But he had already bent down and his fingers had fastened over a small black plastic case. He straightened and extended it to her, in the flat palm of his hand.

'What's this?' he asked.

Jo, almost heady with relief, looked from the small inoffensive rectangle and up into the face of her husband. It was stiff, set with an ominous expression that sent a swift shiver of apprehension down her spine.

'You know what it is,' she said, quietly.

He shook the package slightly, and

the pills rattled in their little plastic bubbles. 'Oh, yes, I know what it is. But I should like to know what it is doing in your handbag.'

'Does that need an explanation, Clay? I have a career. In fact I applied for the senior engineer's job today and I'm sure I'll get it. You can just imagine the response if two months later I leave to have a baby. Redmonds would never employ another woman on site. And who could blame them?'

'I am completely indifferent to Redmonds' policy on the employment of women. I *do* care about this.'

She avoided his eye. 'I'm not ready to give up everything I've worked so hard to achieve to have a family.'

'You don't think,' he said, with a painful, icy calm, 'that it would have been . . . polite . . . to impart that particular piece of information to me?'

'This is ridiculous, Clay. We're grown up, for heaven's sake. Surely you didn't expect me to produce a son and heir nine months to the day of our wedding.'

'A daughter would be equally acceptable.'

'I don't believe this. You never said anything about children when you asked me to marry you. Demanded that I marry you.'

'Forgive me for being somewhat slow-witted, but I thought that marriage was a total commitment. Or don't you love me quite enough to want to bear my children?'

'Love?' The tears were biting at her eyelids now, but she refused to let them fall. When had he ever spoken of love? 'Surely we married for lust, Clay. Isn't that what you said?'

His hands closed tightly on the small package. 'I hadn't realised that you had taken me quite so literally.' His eyes were gem-hard in the evening light and she stepped back, suddenly afraid.

'Going somewhere?' he asked, and he moved swiftly to block her exit.

'I have to get dinner,' she babbled.

'Later.' He let the small packet fall from his hand and caught her wrist, jerking her close. Then with his other hand he began, very slowly, to undress her. 'Right now, I'll settle for lust.'

She fought him, beating at his shoulders in silent fury but he ignored her onslaught, not hurting her, simply holding her in an iron grip until at last she stood panting, her naked breast heaving against a shirt-front from which the buttons had been ripped in her struggles.

'Clay, please!'

'Please what, Jo?' His mouth began a series of lightning raids across her shoulder, while the tip of his thumb grazed a betraying nipple already fiercely to attention. She moaned, an urgent fire kindling deep within her as he touched her, caressed her, played her body with the skill of a virtuoso, until she was tearing feverishly at his clothes.

There was a savage magnificence about their coupling that had nothing to do with love. And when, at long last, it was over, there was no tender rest to be found in Clay's arms. Instead he held her fiercely at arm's length, raking her with eyes numbing in their cold intensity, his teeth bared in a predatory grin.

'Whoever would have guessed, Miss Grant, that beneath that cool exterior there lurked a sleeping tiger?'

She wrenched herself free and fled to the shower, turning it to a biting cold, desperate to cool the hot shame of her own wanton response to him, desperate to hide from those knowing eyes, but his laughter, real or imagined she hardly knew, followed her there, echoing in her head.

After a long time she wrapped herself in a towelling robe and emerged. He was lying back on the pillows, turning the pill case between his fingers.

'Do you still want these?' he asked, without expression.

She was unable to answer. She didn't know what she wanted any more beyond the gentle comfort of his arms. But that was denied her. He rose in one smooth movement from the bed and she dragged her eyes away from the magnificence of his body, wincing as he pressed the package into her palm and wrapped her fingers firmly around it.

'Here, then. But don't take them on my account, sweetheart. I'm going to Canada tomorrow.'

'Canada?'

'That was my news. I thought you would have liked to come with me for a belated honeymoon. But clearly your career has to come first.' He pushed her fringe back from her eyes. 'You are your father's daughter, Jo. Right down to the cement dust in your hair.' She reached for him, wanting to hold him, convince him of her love, but he turned to open the wardrobe and began to throw clothes into a holdall.

Fear stabbed through her. 'You said tomorrow.'

'I'll stay at the airport hotel tonight. What's left of tonight.'

'Clay, please!'

He raised his eyes to hers. 'Sorry, darling. I've had more than enough for one night.' Her breath came in a sharp, cold gasp against her teeth and, apparently satisfied, he zipped the bag closed. 'We'll talk about our marriage when I get back, Jo. In the meantime, perhaps it's time you gave some thought to your priorities.' With that, he walked into the bathroom and closed the door firmly behind him.

5

Joanna was dressed and waiting when he came down into the hall and he glanced at his watch.

'Not going to bed? It's a little early for work, even by your standards.'

'Not at all. The site is working round the clock,' she said, calmly, determined not to be drawn into a game of sniping.

'Well, you'll be able to keep really busy while I'm away,' he said, cruelly, 'without anything as tiresome as a husband to distract you.'

She shook her head. 'I wasn't included in the night-shift rota. Clay — '

'And you stood for that?' His mouth twisted in a mockery of a smile. 'You're slipping. Isn't that some sort of discrimination?'

'I was glad,' she said urgently, seeking to convince him. 'I wanted to be home with you.' He merely raised a disbelieving brow and for a moment she froze. Then she reached for her bag, fumbling for her keys so she wouldn't have to see the cold, hard expression in his eyes. 'I — I dressed because you'll need a lift to the airport.'

'I've already called a taxi. It will be here any moment.' As if to confirm his words a car horn sounded at the gate.

'When will you be home?' she asked, trying desperately not to let him see how much the effort of making polite conversation was costing her.

'I'll let you know.'

Her fragile mask began to slip. 'Can I have your address? A telephone number?' She was reduced to begging and didn't care.

'If there's anything urgent my office can find me.' He opened the door and paused against the dark rectangle of the sky. Then he disappeared into the dark. She wanted to run down the path, chase the headlights' bumpy passage down the lane. Tell him how much she loved him, make him listen to her, promise him anything. But she clung to the doorpost, sinking to the floor, resting her cheek against the cool ancient wood, until the birds roused her with their dawn clamour.

She rose stiff with cold and climbed the stairs. The contents of her bag were still scattered across the floor and she picked them up, stuffing them in anyhow. All except the pills. Those she threw, one by one, into the toilet and flushed them away. She dropped the empty packet into the bin. When Clay came home they would talk, she decided. Thrash it all out. Everything. Then, perhaps, they could pick up the pieces and start again.

The days passed. She missed him so much that it was like a pain. She longed simply to hear the sound of his voice, but he didn't telephone or write and she tried to tell herself that he was right. She needed time to make decisions about her future. But when the phone did ring she ran to answer it, breathless with hope, only to be disappointed.

Her mother invited her over for the weekend and she thought it would help to fill the numbing loneliness. But two days of putting a brave face on for her mother made her wish she had stayed at home where her pallor could remain unremarked upon and she wouldn't have to field carefully couched questions regarding the likelihood of her starting a family.

On Sunday afternoon an urgent summons from Peter was a welcome opportunity to escape.

'Sorry to call you out, Jo,' Peter said, as she arrived. 'But Mike's been rushed to hospital with suspected appendicitis and I've got a family do.'

'It's no problem.'

'Not for you, maybe. But it is for me. You're not supposed to be working the night-shift.'

'That's silly.'

'Yes, I know. I told them at the office that you'd have a fit. I was amazed, frankly, that you took it so calmly.'

Jo shrugged. 'Well, don't worry. I

shan't mention it if you don't.'

But it was a long night and it was with infinite relief that she saw Peter's car turn into the yard. She finished signing the last of the worksheets and almost fell into her car.

'I don't think you should drive, Jo. Come on. I'll give you a lift.'

Peter's face swam above her and she didn't bother to argue. She felt giddy, sick with tiredness, and had almost to be helped to his car.

She woke as the car stopped outside the cottage. 'What?' For a moment she was totally confused. 'Oh, I'm home.'

'Safe and sound.' He leaned across and opened the car door, halting, his face far too close to hers, something uncomfortably close to a leer curving his lips. 'Don't I deserve a reward?' Before she could move he had touched her lips with his own. She pushed him away and began to climb quickly from the car but his voice followed her.

'Well, now I know why you didn't make a fuss about the night-shift.'

'I'm sorry?' Her voice was forbidding.

'That's not a car I'm likely to forget.'

Jo focused on the Aston standing on the gravel driveway, suddenly wide awake at the implications of what she could see. 'It's not what you think, Peter,' she said quickly and opened the gate.

His laughter followed her. 'That rather depends upon what I'm thinking.'

But she hardly heard him as she ran down the path to the cottage. It had all become too silly. She was married, for heaven's sake. She had clung to her father's name for long enough. She wasn't Jo Grant any more. Clay was home and her joy at that fact was an end to all the uncertainties. Nothing was more important than her love for him.

The door opened as she raised her key to the latch and he stood back to let her inside.

'Clay!' she exclaimed and threw her

arms around him. 'I'm so glad you're back.' He made no move to hold her; instead he reached over her head and pushed the door. It shut with a crash behind her and she jumped and stepped back, feeling foolish. 'I'm sorry I wasn't here when you arrived. You must have wondered . . . '

'Must I? Well, you didn't keep me in suspense for very long,' he said evenly. He turned abruptly and left her standing in the hall.

She followed him into the living-room, realising that something was very wrong. 'If I had known you were coming I would have left a message.' He didn't answer, didn't even bother to turn around. 'You said you would let me know when you were coming home.'

He turned then, his eyes wintry. 'How inconvenient that I chose to surprise you.'

'Inconvenient?' she echoed, blankly.

'I did ring your mother when I got home, assuming that you would be there. My father told me you were going there for the weekend when I telephoned him a couple of days ago.'

'You were able to use a telephone, then?' she said, suddenly furious for all the heartache she had endured. 'I thought perhaps you must have lost the use of your dialling finger.'

He ignored this outburst. 'He said you were with your mother,' he repeated. 'So I called her.'

'I was there.'

'Undeniably. Except you left there just after tea on Sunday. Called away to work, she said. She was very convincing, but then, I expect she believed it.'

'I was,' she repeated, helplessly.

'All night, Jo? When I distinctly remember you telling me that you had been excluded from the night-shift.'

Cold apprehension clutched at her insides as she realised what he was implying. 'For heaven's sake, Clay, ask Peter; he'll tell you — '

'Of that I have no doubt. I'm sure he has his own reasons for covering his tracks. A wife, for one. Maybe I'm wrong, but he has the look of a married man. But perhaps she's more forgiving than I am.'

'I have been working for the last twelve hours, Clay. I'm too tired to argue with you.'

'In an expensive silk blouse and a skirt? Pushing credibility just a bit too far, wouldn't you say?'

'I borrowed a pair of overalls from . . .' She stopped. She had done nothing to be ashamed of. Nothing to excuse herself for. 'This is ridiculous. I'm going to have a shower and go to bed. We can talk when you're feeling a little more rational.' She walked quickly away from him and hurried to the stairs, but he followed her.

'If you plan to sleep in my bed, be sure to change the sheets before you leave.' The slashing edge of his voice was like a knife, cutting so deep that nothing could ever stop the pain, bringing her to an abrupt halt on the first rise of the stairs. She turned, her hand clutching at the rail to prevent herself from falling.

'You want me to leave?'

'Oh, yes, Jo. I want you to leave. Before I get home this evening. I'm afraid there's nothing generous in my nature where you are concerned. I won't share.'

The hard, uncompromising planes of his face swam before her. She blinked the tears back. She had been ready to give up everything she had ever wanted to be with Clay Thackeray, but he had told her to go. Leave. And none of it was true. She reached for him, determined to get through to him somehow.

'Don't touch me.' His voice was low. He had not raised it above a polite conversational tone throughout, yet it vibrated with menace. She pulled back her fingers as if she had been burned.

'Clay,' she appealed desperately, making a last attempt to get through. But his face was shuttered, closed to her. He was convinced she had spent the night with Peter Lloyd and nothing she said was going to change his mind. And she would not grovel. If he had so little trust in her, perhaps it was better to end it quickly. A sharp stab of guilt caught in her throat. There had been precious little trust on either side.

Pride was all that remained. Marry in haste, the old adage went, repent at leisure. Well, she had her promotion; that was a start. She would just have to ensure that she had no leisure to waste on regret.

She said nothing — she was no longer capable of speech — and he nodded, as if satisfied that he had made his point, before turning for the door. He stood for a moment in the opening and took a deep breath and, when he turned back, just for a moment her heart flickered back into life.

'I'm sorry, Jo. I should have remembered that when you wake a sleeping tiger you have to stick around to keep it under control.' Then he was gone. She heard the throaty roar of the Aston as it disappeared down the lane. Then there was silence.

She sank to the stairs, her legs unable to hold her, and sat there for a while, quite numb with shock.

The ringing of the telephone brought her to her feet. It might be him, she thought wildly. He might have changed his mind. She reached for the receiver, but the answerphone cut in and she remained motionless, her hand ready to snatch it up at the first sound of his voice. The message ended, the tone sounded.

'Hello, Clay? This is Henry Doubleday. Redmond's found out what you're doing and it's all going to pieces. I think we'd better meet as soon as possible.'

The man hung up. Henry Doubleday. She frowned, trying to clear her clouded brain, to think where she had heard the name before. Then she remembered.

In a sudden panic she flew up the stairs. She packed her clothes, flinging them into suitcases without care. She had to get away, get everything out of the cottage before he returned, because she was never coming back.

She stripped the bed and pushed the linen into the washing machine, then set the programme. He would have to remake it himself, or maybe Mrs Johnson would. It was no longer her concern.

At last it was done and she summoned a taxi. The driver surveyed the quantity of her luggage, the boxes of her possessions and, about to complain, saw Jo's face. He carried them unprotesting to the car. 'Where to, miss?' he asked, finally.

For a moment she couldn't think. Where on earth could she go? To her mother, or her sister? 'To a hotel,' she said, eventually. 'Somewhere reasonable in Woodhurst.' Somewhere to crawl away and lick her wounds in private.

'The Red Lion?'

She nodded. The Red Lion would do as well as anywhere. It no longer mattered where she went.

Joanna pulled sharply at the fingers of the thin leather gloves she used for driving, using them as an escape valve for her anger.

'Late, Peter?' He didn't improve, she thought. He had put on weight, and the smooth tanned lines of his face were beginning to sag. At least out on site he had had some exercise to keep him in trim. She had never been able to understand why Charles Redmond had taken him on to the board. She stood in the open doorway of the boardroom. How like him to have their meeting in the grandeur of the oak-panelled room, where he could demonstrate his new power.

'We were expecting you two hours ago. I suppose you had car trouble?' The sneer in his voice was the final straw. He was convinced that she used her friendship with Charles Redmond to keep her position, to rise steadily up the ladder, despite everything. But now

Charles was dead and he thought she was fair game. Well, she wouldn't go down without a fight.

'If you ever bothered to listen to the weather forecast north of Bristol, Peter, you would know that my site is under four inches of snow. The road across the Beacons was closed at Storey Arms and I had to wait for a police convoy.' She paused to draw breath. 'I finally got to the Severn Bridge just as it closed because of high winds and had to drive up to Gloucester in a two-mile queue of lorries. Now, perhaps you would like to tell me exactly what was so important that I had to be here this afternoon, when I would much rather have been building a snowman!'

'Mr Lloyd sent for you at my request, Miss Grant. I thought it was important that you should meet your new chairman.'

Joanna spun in the direction of the soft, well-modulated voice that even now had the power to make the blood leap in her veins, bringing a flush to her skin and making her heart beat unbelievably fast. She took a step into the room and closed the door. It was him. Sitting at the far end of the long polished table, the window behind him so that his face was in shadow.

'Please come and sit down. I'm sure Mr Lloyd will be happy to fetch a cup of coffee for an old . . . friend.' His eyes gleamed coldly.

'I . . . ' She looked at Peter and then back to her husband. She nodded, helplessly.

She wanted to shout at him, ask him what he thought he was doing to come crashing back into her world when she had finally reached a state where peace seemed a possibility. But if the past two years had given her nothing else, it had given her self-control. She jerked a nervous glance to the secretary's office next door. No. More than self-control. Much more.

He indicated the chair beside him and she walked slowly down the room, her feet sinking soundlessly into the soft carpet. She lowered herself, very carefully, into the chair beside him and stared unseeing at the cup Peter placed in front of her. 'I'm sorry to hear that you have had such a bad journey.'

'You could have rung in,' Peter interjected. 'You have a telephone in your car.'

'It . . . it isn't working.'

Clay made a note on the pad in front of him. 'I see that you've been running the site at Brynglas ever since the project manager went on sick leave.' She nodded silently, a hard knot in the pit of her stomach. 'You're several weeks behind.' He sounded reasonable enough and yet she was sure that something bad was going to happen.

'Yes.'

'Six weeks.' Peter's voice rang with satisfaction.

Clay shot him a silencing glance. 'You are being relieved of that position as from today.'

Her head jerked up then and she faced him. Was the destruction of her career to be his final revenge? 'For what reason?'

'Company restructuring.'

'Are you dissatisfied with my work?' she asked, coldly. 'I will have to ask you to justify any complaints.' She glanced across at Peter. She had been so sure when the summons came that he wanted to tell her in person that he was the new chairman and her days were numbered. She could have fought Peter, but Clay? When had she ever been able to fight him?

There was a tap at the door and the secretary put her head around it. 'I'm sorry to interrupt, gentlemen. Jo, have you got a bag for Alys? Bit of an emergency.'

She caught her breath and glanced quickly at Clay. His face, half-shadowed, was expressionless. She rose. 'I'm sorry, I left it in the car.'

'Give me a key. I'll see to it.'

Clay's voice was shatteringly loud in the silence that followed the woman's departure. 'You've brought your child into the office?'

'What can you expect if you allow women the sort of freedom she's had?'

Peter was unable to hide his triumph.

She turned on him. Anywhere but at the stark blue eyes of her husband. 'What did you expect? Should I have left her on a Welsh hilltop in the care of the site foreman?'

'You should be at home looking after her. The office is not an appropriate place for a baby.' Peter knew that she had had a relationship with Clay and she realised with disgust that he was thoroughly enjoying the situation.

'I'm well aware that you vetoed a crèche facility in the office, Peter. But I'm not your only employee with a baby. You have at least one father who is bringing up a child on his own.'

'Enough!' Clay's voice cut through their bitter exchange. 'I have no interest in your domestic arrangements, but my secretary has better things to do than play nursemaid.' His glance fell on Peter Lloyd. 'I won't keep you.' His voice was dismissive.

He turned to Jo, his eyes holding her as surely as shackles. She wished he would not look at her. It was too painful. The memories, she found, even after all this time, were still too raw.

He finally broke the silence. 'How are you, Joanna?'

'As you see me, Clay.'

'Tired and alone. The lovers soon fell out, it would seem.' His eyes flickered to the doorway through which Peter Lloyd had departed.

She turned angrily. 'I'm tired because I've had a tiring day. And no, Clay, I'm not alone.'

'The situation has a certain irony, wouldn't you say? It must cramp your style considerably. But you've managed to see that your career has not suffered. You still give that your first concern.'

'Not my first, Clay. But I haven't neglected it for the simple reason that I need a job. I don't work for myself any more, Clay. I work for my daughter.'

'But the child's father . . . ' His voice trailed away as if he couldn't bear to say the word.

She caught and held the cry of

anguish in her throat. 'I have never asked him for anything.'

A black scowl darkened his face. 'He should still provide for her. Good God! He knows. He said, just now, that you should be at home with her.'

She wondered if he would believe her if she told him the truth. What he would do. She shuddered involuntarily.

'I think perhaps I had better clear up one thing. Clay. Peter is many things, most of them unspeakable, but he is not the father of my child.'

He stood up so suddenly that she jumped. Then he turned his back to her and walked to the window, staring down into the car park below. When he turned back to face her his mouth was twisted into the semblance of a smile.

'That's the thing with late starters. They are so enthusiastic.'

She had asked for that, but it still hurt and she had taken more than enough punishment for one day. She stood up, carefully gathering her gloves and bag, self-respect requiring that she withdraw in good order before she broke down completely.

'I haven't congratulated you on your appointment as chairman. I rather thought Peter would get the job.'

'I'm sorry to disappoint you.'

She hesitated, wanting to get away, needing to find a dark hole into which she could crawl and lick her wounds. But she had to know why he had come back. 'What are you going to do with Redmonds? Will you break the company up?'

'Break it up?'

'That's what 'restructuring' means, isn't it? Sell off the valuable assets and junk the rest. I helped to stop it the last time you tried, but with Charles gone I don't suppose anybody cares very much. Except the people who will be out of work as a result.'

He was beside her before she could move, his face just inches from her own. 'Just what exactly did you think you were helping to stop?'

She could see the small scar on his

chin where an irate workman had once hit him with a shovel and she felt a certain sympathy with the man. It was so close that if she just moved her weight to her toes she could touch it with her lips. And she longed to. Even after all he had done to her, he still evoked an almost animal response from her.

'Mummy!' she turned to see her daughter racing up the length of the boardroom towards her.

Jo scooped up her daughter and held her tightly. A fair mop-haired creature, a tiny miniature of herself in every respect, except that her bright blue corduroy dungarees echoed eyes that every day were a wrenching reminder of Clay. She turned to him and the child stretched out chubby starfish hands to him.

He stared at her with a look of such hunger that Jo's heart missed a beat and for a moment she thought he would touch the tiny fingers. Then he jerked abruptly away.

'We'll continue this in the morning.' His voice was harsh. 'Please be in my office at nine o'clock.'

'I'll fight you, Clay,' she said fiercely.

He smiled slightly. 'I look forward to that battle.' When she made no answer he walked to the door and opened it. 'It will be interesting to see what weapons you can muster. After all, you sold your shares to Charles two years ago.'

She had hoped to bluff him. Hoped he didn't know that. But it seemed he knew everything, except that she loved him and that Alys was his daughter. 'Nine o'clock. Don't be late.'

'If you're going to fire me, Clay, I'd rather you did it now. There's no need to dramatise it any further.'

'Your preferences are no concern of mine and your . . . daughter is nearly asleep.'

She looked at the fair head nestling on her shoulder. 'It's been a long day.'

'How do you manage?' Surprised at the edge of concern in his voice, she raised her eyes to his.

'The same way that thousands of other women manage, Clay. Childminders. Family. Taking her to work when, like today, everything else fails.'

Then he said, brutally, as if regretting his sudden lapse into humanity, 'I thought that you were far too careful to fall into that trap.'

'We all make mistakes, Clay.' She stroked the child's head and added almost to herself, 'At least I managed to do one thing right.' His sharp intake of breath brought her back to reality. 'I must go.'

'Yes. And please make alternative arrangements for tomorrow. This isn't a nursery.'

★ ★ ★

Her mother fussed over them both, asking no questions. It wasn't until Alys was asleep and Jo was curled up in her dressing-gown in front of the fire that she broke the news.

'Clay's back.' Jo sipped her cocoa.

'He's the new chairman of Redmonds.' Her mother's unexpected imprecation sent her eyebrows rocketing.

'You'll resign, of course.'

'I may not have to.'

'Oh, darling, he'd never have the nerve to sack you!'

'They call it restructuring these days.'

'If I get hold of him, he'll be the one . . .'

'No, Mum. Please. It's all over and forgotten. For the moment he's my boss. I'm seeing him first thing in the morning. When I know what he's got in mind, then I can make decisions about the future.'

'You won't listen to my advice?'

'No need, I think I can guess it. Run away?'

'Hard and fast. He hurt you, Jo. I don't know how because you never saw fit to confide in me, but I saw what it did to you. You can't go through that again, and besides, you've Alys to think of.' She stiffened. 'Would he try and get custody of her?'

'No.' Her mother deserved some sort of explanation. She had never asked what had gone wrong, never criticised. She had been proved right and that had apparently been enough. She didn't need to say 'I told you so' and for that Jo had been grateful. 'Clay is under the impression that Alys is the result of . . . of . . . a fling.' She watched with a kind of awful fascination as a tear fell into her cup.

'A what?'

'When he went to Canada.'

'The man's a fool. And so are you if you want to keep him ignorant. He's only got to look at the child — '

'Apparently not. He saw her today.'

'But her eyes, Jo!'

'I wouldn't have taken her to the office if I'd known he would be there. But it didn't matter. He never noticed. And there's no reason for him to see her again.' She looked up. 'Will you look after her tomorrow?'

'If you moved back home you would never have to worry about babysitters again. You could just get on with your career. You've done so well.'

'Have I?'

'It's not the time for doubts. Your marriage was just a blip. An aberration. But it's out of your system now and you're moving on.' She frowned. 'You will be careful, won't you? He's a dangerous man. Strong, wilful.'

'Yes, Mum. I'll be careful.'

★ ★ ★

'Don't fuss, Jo. I can look after Alys. I'm far more worried about you. That man . . . ' She regarded her daughter with concern. 'Why don't you just take leave in lieu of notice?'

'I can't do that.'

Her mother shrugged philosophically. 'No, I suppose not. You never did do things the easy way.' She looked admiringly at her daughter's clothes. 'At least you're going down with all flags flying.'

Jo checked her reflection in the

156

mirror. The suit, with its plain, old gold, collarless jacket and soft skirt in a bold abstract print of white and black and the same old gold, had come from her sister's boutique. She wound a scarf of the same material around her neck and nodded.

'Yes, Mum. All flags.' Today was definitely not a day for jeans.

'Miss Grant?' She paused in Reception an hour later and looked at the man who had spoken to her.

'Yes.'

'I'm from Pentagon Motors. I've come for your car. Could I have your keys, please?'

She looked at the keys, still in her hand, and the Pentagon key fob. The leasing company for all the company cars. She had heard of such things happening: being sacked and having to get a bus home. The modern equivalent of having your sword broken and the epaulettes ripped from your uniform.

'It's . . . I haven't . . . I need to clear it out.'

He shrugged. 'If you insist. Can you do it straight away? I haven't much time.'

She stiffened. 'Of course.'

She led the way to the car park and unlocked the car. There wasn't much. Some maps. Driving shoes. She bent to pick them up and discovered a feeding cup that Alys had dropped.

'What about the boot?'

'No. It's empty.' The man was looking expectantly at her. 'Here.' She handed him the keys and he climbed in, driving away with the sort of fierce bravado that some men seemed to feel was necessary in the presence of a woman. Or maybe he was just as embarrassed as she was. She walked back into the office and up to the first floor.

His secretary waved her to the door. 'Go straight in. He saw you arrive and he's waiting for you.'

So, he had watched the little performance in the car park. She straightened her back and opened the door. He looked up briefly from his writing block and motioned her to a seat.

'Sit down, Joanna. I won't be a minute.' He carried on writing in his bold, incisive hand, giving her a moment to notice the fine sprinkle of grey hair at his temple. Then he threw down his pen and sat back. 'Would you like some coffee?'

'No, thank you. I can do without the niceties. I'm not prepared to sit and let you gloat, Clay. You've humiliated me enough for one day. Say what you have to and then let me go.'

'Humiliated?' He frowned. 'In what way?'

She stood up. 'Do you want me to make it easy for you and resign?'

'For heaven's sake sit down. You never used to indulge in hysterics.'

'I've never been sacked before.'

He fixed her with a glare that riveted her to her seat. 'I haven't asked you to come all this way to sack you, as you so inelegantly put it.'

'Then why have you taken my car?'

'Taken your car?' He looked at her blankly.

'Did you enjoy the performance? I understand from Mrs Gregg that you watched from your window.'

'What the hell are you talking about?'

'I was mugged in Reception by a driver from the leasing company. You might at least have waited until afterwards . . .'

Light at last dawned. 'You complained last night of a faulty car phone. Pentagon were asked to fit a replacement as soon as possible. I had no idea they were coming today.'

'Car phone?' She stared at him. 'Then why on earth didn't the man say?'

'I imagine he thought you knew. And now we've cleared up one misunderstanding we'd better move on to the next. I have brought you in from the site, Jo, because I want you working here. In the office.'

'No!'

She might never have spoken. 'You've proved yourself in every possible way to be competent, hard-working and reliable. Even in the most trying circumstances. Reading between the lines of your weekly reports, the last few months at Brynglas cannot have been easy. And, despite Lloyd's attempts to blacken you, I am well aware that, when you took over, the job was ten weeks adrift.' He sat back in his chair and regarded her from beneath hooded lids. 'He's very anxious to get rid of you, did you know?'

'I'm not surprised.'

He waited for some sort of explanation but she said nothing more. He had no doubt already made up his own mind about why Peter would want to be rid of her and nothing she said would change it.

'No, I don't suppose you are. But he is going to be disappointed. However, if you're going to progress further in your career you need some management experience.'

Progress? What on earth did that mean? 'And if I prefer to stay out on site?'

'At the moment you have no choice in the matter.'

'I could leave Redmonds.'

'Not so easy at the moment. You did say you needed a job?' He regarded her thoughtfully. 'I wonder what sort of reference Lloyd would dream up for you?'

'He wouldn't dare!'

'You're prepared to take the risk?' He was provoking her deliberately, but she was determined not to rise to the bait. Apparently satisfied with her silence, he continued. 'You've proved you can do the job out there at the sharp end. Now it's time to demonstrate that there's more to Miss Joanna Grant than reinforced concrete. Or are you afraid to try?'

6

Clay was challenging her head-on, forcing her to make a decision that would affect the rest of her life. In daring her to stay and face him he was instituting a war of nerves, and Joanna wasn't about to turn tail and run. She met the mocking question in his eyes and forced her lips into an answering smile.

'What exactly are you offering, Clay?'

A glint of satisfaction lit those seemingly bottomless blue depths and her smile faltered. It was hard enough to sit opposite the man she loved so much that each day it was a physical pain which could only be defeated by working herself until she dropped. His father had said, the day they were married, that Clay always got exactly what he wanted. Now she wondered with a qualm of unease just exactly what he wanted from her.

'I have a job for you in the planning department.'

'Planning!' At her arrogant gesture of dismissal his face darkened.

'You can have your say when I've finished. Be quiet and listen to what I'm offering before you dismiss my proposition out of hand.' His voice rattled against her and, stunned into silence by his blazing arrogance, she found herself doing exactly what she was told. When at last he had finished he leaned back in his chair. 'Now, you may speak.'

'I . . . hardly know what to say.'

'Well, I have achieved something.' His mouth finally twisted in the semblance of a smile. 'Does that mean you're tempted by my proposition?'

Of course she was tempted. He knew her too well, knew exactly what would hold her, and he had held out the sweetest plum. But first there would be six months in the planning office, every day spent under his eye, at his beck and call, subject to his whim. Her mother's advice to run as hard and fast as she could rang loudly in her ears. She needed time to think and so she countered his question with one of her own.

'This is a long-term proposition, Clay. What happened to the restructuring?'

'The restructuring?' For a moment his dark brows drew together in a frown, then he leaned towards her and instinctively she edged back. 'The restructuring is on hold, Jo.' Even across the vastness of his desk the threat was clear. 'Until I have your answer.'

For a long time she didn't say anything. Somewhere a telephone was ringing. There was a burst of laughter in the corridor. Outside these four walls, she thought, people were going about their business quite unaware of this quiet drama taking place in Clay's office that could affect all their lives.

'How long do I have to think about

it? she said, at last.'

'Not long. Henry Doubleday will be here at eleven. You've met, I believe?' he said. 'I shall have to know by then.' His eyes gave her no clue to his thoughts. And when he spoke his voice held none of the warmth that for a few weeks, a painfully few, had had the power to bring her total happiness. 'Last time I made a bid for this company, Jo, you thwarted me. Now I'm going to make you pay for that.'

She felt her blood run to ice. The ruthless man sitting opposite her was her husband. The father of her child. The man she had loved. A catch in her throat caught her by surprise; still loved, although he had broken her heart beyond mending. And he was going to punish her for something she had never done. She held herself very still. It was vital that she didn't show any emotion, then at least she would prevent a total defeat. She raised her clear grey eyes to meet his. 'You were going to destroy Redmonds,' she said, with only the faintest betraying tremor in her voice. 'You told me yourself you have no interest in mere 'concrete' any more.'

'It has its uses. I'm always happy to gather another profitable company under my wing.'

'Even if you had to marry me to make certain?' No wonder it had been so easy for him to walk away. Perhaps he had never intended to stay.

'My mistake. But now I'm giving you a chance to redeem yourself. Once again the fate of Redmonds is in your hands, Joanna.' He glanced at his watch. 'And time is running out. What shall I do? Save it or throw it away?'

'You're the consultant, Clay. What would you advise?'

'I'm in the happy position of being unable to lose.' He shrugged and leaned back in his chair. 'The choice is all yours.'

'There doesn't seem to be much choice involved. I cannot just sit back and allow you to throw Redmonds to the wolves. I accept your offer.'

His smile was chilling. 'I thought I could rely upon you for blind loyalty to your company. You should try it on people occasionally.'

She blenched. 'Not totally blind,' she said, desperately. 'There are two conditions, Clay.'

'What makes you believe you're in a position to make conditions?' His cynical demand brought a flush to her cheeks but she refused to back down.

'I'm making these.' He raised a condescending brow and nodded for her to continue. 'If we're to work in the same building, Clay, the past must be forgotten.'

A vein beat fiercely at his temple. 'Have you forgotten it? Have there been so many other men in your life that you can blot out memories of what it was like to lie in my arms?'

She hadn't forgotten. Not for a moment. Even as he spoke she felt the fiery colour rush to her cheeks as her body responded to the pictures his words evoked. Apparently satisfied with the effect of his words, he made a dismissive gesture. 'You said two conditions.'

'I want to buy back my shares.'

A faint smile curved his lips. 'Can you afford them?'

'I still have the money from the original sale.' Money that she would need to buy a home for Alys. It had been a rash demand, a symptom of her need to patch up an ego battered by his insolent demands. Clay Thackeray was altogether too much in command and she wanted to see him stopped in his tracks. But he was unmoved.

'You once told me that you knew nothing about business, Jo. I think perhaps the shares are safer in my hands for the moment.'

'And my other condition?' she persisted desperately.

For a moment their eyes locked. Then he stood up. 'I'll think about it.'

She rose to her feet. 'Make sure you do.'

He nodded. 'If you insist. But it might be safer to let sleeping dogs lie.

Now, I'll take you down to Planning and get you settled in.' He reached for her arm and she jerked nervously at his touch, afraid of the power he still had to raise her pulse-rate, but he tightened his grip, ignoring her reaction. It was just chemistry, she told herself. Nothing else. But it made no difference to the way her pulse raced.

'I know my way,' she said quickly.

'I don't doubt it.' And she knew there was no further point in protesting. With Clay there never was. 'You'll be wanting your things from Brynglas. I imagine you've quite a lot of stuff there?' he said, conversationally, as she allowed him to lead her down the stairs.

'Quite a lot,' she agreed dully. Most of it belonged to Alys.

'Shall I have someone collect it for you? Or would you like to borrow a transit van and fetch it yourself?'

'I have to go back. I can't just abandon Mrs Rhys without a word of thanks after all she's done for me and Alys.'

'You'll need to take two days, I imagine?' His voice remained light, only the tightening of his jaw muscles suggesting any emotion.

'Yes.'

He stopped, forcing her to do the same. 'Will your mother take care of . . . Alys?'

'Yes. She'll be happy to.'

He seemed surprised, and it was a relief to reach the planning department, although when he had gone and she was able to think clearly again she realised that he hadn't in fact agreed to either of her conditions.

★　★　★

'Well?' Her mother had waited until Alys was in bed before she began her interrogation.

'I've a new job. In Planning. I'll be working at the office for a while.'

'The clothes must have made the hoped-for impression, then.'

'What? Oh, I suppose so.'

'Although it doesn't sound quite your cup of tea. Are you really going to take it?'

'It won't be like working in the office when I was expecting Alys.' Jo pulled a face at the memory of the weeks stuck behind a drawing-board. 'I'll be working on a major new project and then Clay's promised me the job of agent for the temporary works.'

'Good lord!' She saw the brief gleam of triumph in her mother's eyes, but it was quickly extinguished. 'And just what does he want in return?' she asked.

'Nothing!' Even to her own ears she sounded a little fierce, as if she was trying to convince herself. 'It's a fantastic opportunity, that's all,' she added, less emphatically.

'So you'll be staying on?'

'You could sound a little more enthusiastic. I thought you'd be pleased. Can you put up with us for a few weeks until I can find somewhere to live?'

'As long as you like, you know that.' Her mother's look was measuring. 'But

I'm still not sure that it's wise. Can you cope?'

'Cope?'

'Come on, Jo. You toughed it out, never let the mask drop, but I saw what it did to you when you split up with Clay. Can you really manage to forget that?' There was no answer. 'Can he?' she added, as an afterthought.

'Clay and I are history.'

'So are Antony and Cleopatra.' She shrugged. 'Oh, well, it's another step on the ladder. Just remember that I warned you. Stay clear of him.'

'I'll remember. Oh, I'm borrowing a transit van to go to Brynglas and collect all our stuff. Will you look after Alys, or shall I take her with me?'

'Leave her with me. I can spoil her rotten for a couple of days without you scowling at me.'

* * *

Jo wrapped up in warm black dungarees and a bright red ski jacket against the long journey. A horn sounded in the road and she grabbed her bag, kissed Alys and hugged her mother.

'There's the driver. I'll get back tonight if I can. It depends on the weather.'

Jo hurried down to the gate and opened the van door. 'Clay!' She took an involuntary step back, then managed to pull herself together sufficiently to offer a smile. 'How kind of you to bring the van yourself.'

'It was no trouble. Your mother is waving, Jo. Do you think she's seen me? Shall I wave back?' She looked around and saw her mother at the window.

'No!' If her mother saw Clay she would be sure to think the worst. She waved herself and he pulled his mouth down in a provoking little smile.

'Very touching. Now get in. I'm in a hurry.'

She swung herself up and fastened her seatbelt. 'So why are you here?' she asked, as they headed for the main road. 'Surely we're not that short of drivers.' Then she frowned as he took the slip-road to the motorway. 'This isn't the way back to the office.'

'How perceptive. I was going up to Brynglas anyway. It seemed an unnecessary waste of fuel for us to travel separately. And as your belongings won't fit in the Aston — '

'You're going . . . ?' She turned on him. 'You planned this deliberately! How could you?'

'Easily. You didn't think I brought you into the office out of the kindness of my heart, did you? You'll have your promotion at the end of it, but in the meantime don't expect to enjoy yourself. Particularly not with your male colleagues.'

'You haven't got a heart!' she gasped.

'No?' His mouth clamped down hard for a moment. Then he managed a smile. 'No. Not any more. But I do remember what it was like to have one.'

'Take me home right now!' she demanded.

He ignored her and she glanced

helplessly around. They were hurling relentlessly down the motorway. It was miles to the next services and she doubted that he would stop even if she begged him.

'Why have you done this?' she demanded. Then colour washed her face. She couldn't, wouldn't put into words the disquieting thoughts spinning around her head. 'What do you want from me?'

'Why should I want anything? I've already had everything on offer.' His brows rose at her involuntary imprecation.

'I — I don't want to go to Brynglas with you.'

'That's no surprise. I'm sure you have plenty of loose ends to tie up that I'll get in the way of. But it's too far for you to drive both ways in a day and I have no intention of allowing you the luxury of an overnight stop. With two of us to drive we can come back tonight.'

'There's precious little luxury at Brynglas,' she snapped.

'We'll see.'

For a while they drove in silence as they negotiated the busy stretch of the M4, but as the traffic thinned he began to ask her about the job. He was so matter-of-fact and businesslike in his questioning that soon she was responding quite naturally.

'It must have been difficult for you,' he said finally. 'Since the project manager took to drinking whisky for breakfast, in preference to tea.'

She stared at him. He was very well informed. She had never said anything. Never even hinted at the problem. 'I never shared breakfast with him, so I couldn't say.'

'No?' She refused to dignify the suggestion with an answer and he shrugged. They were approaching the bridge and he took the slip-road. 'But speaking of breakfast reminds me that it was a very long time ago.'

She glanced at her watch. 'It's rather early for lunch.'

'Not too late for a second breakfast,

though.' He pulled up in the services car park and turned to her. 'It's a long time since we shared breakfast, Joanna. But I'm willing to take the risk if you are.'

'Risk?' she asked, defiantly. 'What risk?'

He jumped down and came around to her door and opened it. 'Who can say?'

'Clay!' she warned and suddenly felt very alone with him.

'Well?' he laughed softly. 'Are you going to join me? Or are you just going to sit there and wish you had?'

'I'm going to join you, of course.'

He lifted her down and for a moment stood with his hands around her waist. It would have been so easy to put her arms around his neck and kiss him. Despite everything she still wanted to. There was still that instant attraction between them, like iron filings to a magnet. Instead she pulled back, lifted her chin and tightened her coat around her to keep out the biting wind. And anything else that was trying to get in.

'In fact, I'm very hungry,' she said, with a bravado she was far from feeling.

They piled their plates with food and went to sit at a window overlooking the Severn. The huge towers of the bridge stood clear of a low mist that enveloped the estuary, giving a magical air to the view.

'I've always loved this bridge. It's quite beautiful when you can't see the lorries and the toll booths.'

'Beautiful?' Clay regarded the bridge without enthusiasm. 'It's functional, up to a point. But not quite my idea of beauty.' He turned to face her. 'Not that I should be surprised. We manage to differ about most things.'

'Managed, Clay. Past tense.' She bent her attention very firmly to her food but he hadn't finished.

'I'm having some difficulty with our agreement, Joanna.'

'You're not trying hard enough.' But suddenly her appetite had gone.

He reached out and captured her hand, holding it when she would have pulled free to escape the instant fire of his touch. He rubbed idly at the plain gold band he had slipped on to her finger the day they were married. When he looked up, his eyes were wintry. 'You seem to have managed well enough.'

'It takes practice,' she told him with all the chill she could muster and jerked her hand free.

They arrived at Brynglas shortly before twelve and Mrs Rhys hurried from the farmhouse to meet her as she stepped stiffly from the van.

'Come in, *cariad*. Out of the cold.'

Clay stayed in the van. 'I'll be back later. If you can have everything ready to load we'll start straight back.' He frowned. 'I thought you said it was under a pile of snow up here?'

'That was last week,' Mrs Rhys told him. 'It's rained since then. But the snow will be back soon enough.'

'Do you want me to come with you?' Jo asked. 'You don't know the way.'

'I'll find it. You've enough to do here.' He drove away.

She spent several hours packing, then dismantled the cot and began to carry everything down the narrow stairs. It took longer than she expected and when Mrs Rhys suggested something to eat she was more than happy to accept.

Afterwards she settled her rent and gave her the present she had brought, a huge printed Liberty scarf and a pair of black leather gloves. Then they sat by the fire to wait for Clay.

'She's like him, your little one,' Mrs Rhys said finally. 'About the eyes.'

Jo frowned. Mrs Rhys knew nothing about her past relationship with Clay, yet she had seen in an instant the likeness between them. 'We're not . . . together, Mrs. Rhys. Clay has taken over the company I work for, that's all.'

'Well, there's a pity.'

'I'd rather you didn't mention anything.'

She glanced up. 'No. I see. It's dark. I'd better draw the curtains.'

Jo glanced anxiously at the clock from time to time. It was nearly six o'clock when the crunching sound of tyres on gravel sent her rushing to the window.

Mrs Rhys let him in and ushered him to the fire. 'Sit there and warm yourself. I'll get you some soup.'

'Is it always this cold here?' he demanded, as he rubbed his hands vigorously before the flames.

Jo grinned. 'Stick around. It's only November; the best is yet to come.' She left him to his soup and started loading the van, hurrying to get out of the icy wind. 'It's all done. I think we'd better get going, Clay. It's started to rain.'

'I've made you a flask, Jo,' said Mrs Rhys before they left. 'You might be glad of something hot.'

'Bless you.' She hugged the woman. 'I'll bring Alys back in the summer to see you.'

'Come up for the shearing, *cariad*. She'll love it.' She smiled at Clay. 'You'll all be welcome.'

Jo held her breath, but Clay apparently read no special meaning into the

182

words and merely thanked the woman for her hospitality.

'I'll drive,' Jo volunteered.

'No. I'll take this stretch. You can have it when we get to the motorway.' For a moment she considered arguing; she knew the roads up in the hills far better than he did. But he had claimed the driving seat and fastened his seatbelt. 'Come on,' he said, impatiently. She felt an odd reluctance to surrender herself to his mercy once more. She glanced back at Mrs Rhys, standing in the square of light in the doorway that somehow represented safety. Then she raised her hand and climbed in.

He fired the engine and, avoiding as many potholes as possible, left the farmyard. Once he had negotiated the narrow lane they might have been the only people left on earth.

They had been travelling for twenty minutes or so, Clay taking it rather more slowly in the dark, when the rain turned quite suddenly to snow. It wasn't settling much on the roads, but the hillsides rapidly began to whiten and the huge flakes flinging themselves out of the darkness and swirling in the headlights made it difficult to tell where the road ended and the rocky hillside began.

'Should we turn back?' Jo asked, anxiously.

He glanced at her. 'We should be all right . . . ' She shouted a warning as a sheep loomed suddenly out of the darkness and halted, panic-stricken, in the headlights. Clay swerved to avoid hitting it and there was the ominous sound of tearing metal from underneath the van. With a muffled curse he turned off the engine and jumped down to see what the damage was.

'Well?' she demanded.

He got up and brushed the snow from his knees. 'I can't tell without a torch, but I don't think it's good. I can hear something dripping.' He sounded remarkably sanguine, she thought irritably, and looked around. There was not a light to be seen and they hadn't passed another vehicle since they left the farm. She saw him grin in the light from the headlamps. 'Thank goodness for Mrs Rhys and her flask. I have a feeling that we may need it before morning.'

'Morning?' The prospect of a night alone in his company was daunting. 'Surely we can try and get to a garage?'

'I don't think we'll be going anywhere. Get back in. There's no point in getting any colder until I've found the torch.' She complied without demur. The snow had wet her cheeks and the wind was cutting viciously. She rubbed them, already shivering. 'What's the chance of some other vehicle coming along before morning?' he asked.

'Not very high,' she was forced to admit. 'This is a forestry road. Another few weeks and you won't be able to move for rally drivers, but right now it's a bit off the beaten track.' She glanced out at the swirling blizzard. 'And let's be honest, if you didn't have to go somewhere, would you venture out on a night like this?'

'Frankly, no. In fact I can't think what I am doing out on a night like this when I could be sitting in front of Mrs Rhys's fire.'

'I'm sorry.' She began to shake.

'Oh, come on, Jo.' He put his arms around her. 'It's not that bad.' His arms were strong and his voice convincing and she felt safe pressed up against the warmth of his chest.

'Isn't it?' She looked up and for one giddy moment thought that perhaps it wasn't.

He grinned. 'I'm sure I can think of something to do that will keep us warm.' With a shock she recollected where she was. And just who had his arms around her. There was no safety there. He laughed softly as she jerked back, but he made no effort to restrain her. 'No? In that case I'd better summon assistance.' He produced a portable telephone from his jacket and punched in a number.

'How long?' she asked, when he had finished.

'They said twenty minutes.'

'They always say twenty minutes,' she said dismissively. 'How long really?'

'I would say a more realistic estimate is likely to be nearer three or four hours.'

Her heart sank as she recognised the truth in what he said. 'Maybe we could do something ourselves,' she suggested.

'What exactly?'

'Unless we look we won't know,' she said, crossly, and opened the glove compartment. 'There's a torch in here.' She flicked it on and handed it to him.

'Oh, no. If you're that keen you can come and hold the wretched thing for me.' She didn't wait for a second invitation. She opened the door and quickly clambered down. The road was ankle deep in slushy, semi-liquid snow. Clay swore as he skidded on the surface and called a warning back to her. But it was too late. One foot went from under her and before she could save herself she was over the edge and rolling down the snow-covered hill.

'Jo!' She lay for a moment in the dark, breathless and too winded to reply. 'Jo, for heaven's sake answer me!' His anxious voice drifted down to her, but all she could do was lie quite still while she struggled to regain her breath. It was the sound of his feet crashing and slithering down the hillside that jerked her into movement.

'I'm all right,' she managed to croak. 'For goodness' sake stay there.' But he didn't, coming to a halt beside her, showering her with more wet snow, most of which seemed to find its way inside her jacket and down the back of her neck. She was still clinging desperately to the torch and now he eased it away from her numb fingers and flashed it quickly over her.

'Have you broken anything?' He felt urgently at her legs and arms.

She shook her head. 'No, just a few bruises. You should have stayed up there. Now we both have to get back up.' She shivered convulsively.

'Let me worry about that.' He put his arms around her waist and lifted her to her feet. For a moment everything spun giddily and she clung helplessly to him.

'Put your arms around my neck,' he commanded. Slowly, almost mesmerised by the force emanating from his powerful body, she obeyed, linking her fingers behind his head, the warmth of his skin giving her strength. Then he swung her up into his arms and carried her back up the hillside. Once he stumbled on a snow-covered rock and swore viciously.

She lifted her head from his shoulder. 'I can manage, Clay. Put me down.' But he took no notice, holding her closer if anything. And she was glad. Ridiculously, stupidly glad.

It was warmer inside the van, out of the wind, but already the temperature was dropping as the engine quickly cooled. He held her for a moment, cradling her on his lap until the trembling began to lessen.

'I'm sorry, Clay. I feel so stupid!' she muttered into the wet cloth of his jacket.

'With good reason,' he said, softly.

Something in his voice made her look up and she saw with a shock that his hair was sticking wetly to his forehead. 'You're soaking. Oh, lord!' she moaned. 'What a mess. I'll get a towel.'

The need to do something for him put strength back into her limbs and she scrambled into the back of the van and tore at the tape on the boxes with her numb fingers until she found one containing her linen. She pulled out her quilt and sheets and found her towels at the bottom. She handed one to him, quite suddenly unable to meet his eyes. He held it for a moment then he made an exasperated sound.

'You've cut your hand. Here, let me.' He took her hand and wrapped one of the towels around a cut that was beginning to ooze blood.

'I c-can't feel a thing,' she said, then gasped through her shivers as he pulled her against him and began to rub hard at her hair with a towel.

'Now get out of these wet things,' he said. Before she could object he had peeled off her coat and begun to unfasten the clips of her dungarees.

'No!' she protested, but they were sticking wetly against her legs and the snow melting inside her collar was beginning to run down her back.

'You never used to be so shy, Joanna. If you don't get them off you'll freeze.' She made no further protest as he undressed her, lifting each foot obediently at his command, trying not to think about his hands as they brushed against her, his fingers on her skin as he peeled off her sweater. But when he began to rub her vigorously with the towel it was more than the cold that was making her shake.

'Stop. Please stop,' she begged.

'Sure?' His voice was harsh as he wrapped her in the quilt, holding it firmly around her for a moment until she had the wit to grab at it. Then he began to dry his own hair. For a moment she watched him, helplessly mesmerised as she remembered the days, pitifully few of them, when she could have done that for him. 'Pour yourself some coffee.' His voice, sharp, intimidating in the confines of the van, made her start, bringing her sufficiently to her senses to turn away as he pulled off soaking trousers.

It's just chemistry, she reminded herself. Nothing else. The way that dynamite was just chemistry. Jo sipped at the steaming coffee, but, no matter how hard she tried to control them, her teeth wouldn't stop rattling. She watched as he flattened one of the boxes and covered it with her sheets to made a bed of sorts.

'You should be warmer here. Lie down.' She was beyond argument and he lay down beside her, covering them both with the quilt, immediately disappearing under its folds to rub some life back into her legs, peeling off her damp socks to work on her feet. 'Stop, p-please!' she begged, as his touch kindled more than heat. But it seemed forever before he surfaced and every inch of her was glowing with a painful fire.

'Warmer?' She nodded. He rolled on to his back and closed his eyes. 'Your turn.' She swallowed. The thought of deliberately reaching out to touch him was so disturbing that for a moment she didn't think she would be able to do it. But she had to because it was her fault. If she hadn't insisted on looking at the van they would both still be dry. Tentatively at first, and then with more urgency as she felt how cold he was, she chafed at his legs and feet.

'That's enough!' His voice was ragged and before she could object he had put his arm around her and pulled her close. She lay rigid in his arms, knowing the slightest movement would be enough to send them both out of control. So she stayed very still, her ear pressed against the hard wall of his chest, listening to the steady, even thumping of his heart competing with the rising noise of the wind as a thousand memories, brought to vivid life by his closeness, fought for space in her brain. Then a sudden fierce gust shook the transit and she let out a cry of alarm.

Clay crooned softly as she clung to him, holding her tightly while he murmured soft comfort-words into her hair.

'Clay, I'm frightened. Will we freeze to death?'

He lifted his head and in the eerie light reflecting from the snow she could see his eyes. 'No. We won't freeze.' Then he closed them and she saw nothing at all as his mouth descended, blocking out the faint light, the cold, the emptiness.

She caught the warm familiar scent of his skin, and as his fingertips stroked very gently across her neck her lips parted in an involuntary gasp of longing. For a moment the world hung in the balance.

7

For a moment only. Very slowly Joanna drew back from the abyss, gently disengaging herself from the temptations of Clay's arms. His grip tightened and she froze.

'I — can't, Clay,' she whispered.

'No?' His lips teased her throat and she swallowed hard, fighting the desire that blazed like a match struck in the darkness, holding herself rigid against the sweet need to draw close and find comfort in his arms. He raised his head and stared at her for a moment that seemed to last forever.

'I can't,' she repeated, helplessly.

He released her abruptly and sat up. She longed to call him back to her, longed for him to hold her again. But it was time for her to be strong. She had to be strong for Alys.

He turned his back on her. 'If you've

any clothes in those suitcases behind you, this would be a good moment to put them on.'

For just a moment she considered trying to explain. Alys had been denied the joy of a complete family. She had no father and there would be no brothers and sisters. What she did have, what Jo gave her gladly, was the right to expect her mother to think of her first, always before herself.

His back, however, did not invite conversation. Shivering, she left the warmth of the quilt and in the dim light from the cab found a tracksuit and some socks. Dressed, she felt less vulnerable, and she hunted until she found an old pair of men's socks that she wore in her Wellingtons and a sweat-shirt of her father's.

'Will these fit you?' she asked doubtfully. He took the sweater without a word and pulled it on, straining it severely across the shoulders. The socks were better and she had a sudden uncomfortable feeling that they might once have been his. But he said nothing. Instead he pulled the cover over him and turned on his side. For a moment she sat hugging her knees, wondering what on earth to do.

'Try and get some sleep, Jo. It'll be a long night.'

Sleep. She would have laughed if she hadn't felt quite so much like crying. She wouldn't, couldn't lie beside him. Then, with a sudden jolt, she realised it wasn't necessary.

'Clay!'

He turned over and stared up at her. 'What is it, Jo? Changed your mind?' he asked, roughly.

Grateful for the darkness that hid her burning cheeks, she ignored his crude gibe. 'We can use your telephone to call Mrs Rhys. She'll come and fetch us in the Land Rover. At least we won't freeze to death.'

'We won't freeze to death here,' he said, heavily.

'Please!' At her soft plea he sighed, but sat up and retrieved the phone from his jacket.

'What's her number?' he asked, and punched it in as she repeated it. 'It's unobtainable,' he said, after a moment. 'Could the wind have brought down the line?'

Jo bit her lip. 'It could have. Try again; maybe you misdialled.' She repeated the number again and he shook his head and held out the receiver for her to listen.

'Nice try, Jo. But you're stuck with me. Now, try and get some sleep.'

She lay down then, trying not to touch him, although in the confined space that was difficult. Then he turned over and put his arm around her and she stiffened. But there was nothing threatening about the gesture; he was offering simple human contact and she found herself relaxing into the welcome warmth of his body.

* * *

'Jo?' The sound of his voice and the sudden coldness at her back woke her and she struggled stiffly to sit up.

'What is it?'

'The breakdown truck.' A light swung vivid flashes of yellow across his face in the darkness and he grimaced as he hauled on damp trousers. 'Better get your things together,' he advised, before jumping down to explain the situation to their rescuer.

The driver of the rescue vehicle was horribly cheerful. 'Good morning, Mrs Thackeray.' She jerked involuntarily at the unfamiliar sound of the name and glanced at Clay but his face was unreadable, all yellow and black shadows. With any luck hers would be the same. 'Sorry we've been so long. I was telling your husband that it's been a bad night all over. It seems to be clearing up now, though.' The moon made a brief appearance from behind the clouds and for a moment everything sparkled. 'Why don't you go and get in the cab? It's warm in there and we'll soon have this loaded up.'

Eventually the van was loaded on to

the trailer and Clay climbed into the front with the driver.

'Would you like a sandwich, Mrs Thackeray?' he said, leaning back and offering her a plastic box full of thickly cut cheese sandwiches.

Clay threw a hard look at her, daring her, it seemed, to contradict the name. 'No, thank you.' She remembered to smile. At least she hoped what she was doing was smiling.

'Mr Thackeray?' he offered. Clay shook his head.

The driver took them to a garage where Clay arranged for the van to be repaired and hired another one to get them home. They transferred her boxes and bags in total silence and finally set off with Clay at the wheel.

They drove through the snowy darkness for miles and the silence stretched endlessly between them. Jo couldn't think of a way to break it, and anyway Clay seemed lost in thought, hardly aware of her existence.

At the bridge he headed for the

services, cutting off her protest that they should push on. 'I need some coffee to keep me awake.'

'Oh!' She felt stupid and in an effort to make amends she suggested breakfast. 'You must be hungry.'

'Yes. I'm hungry.' He stared at her for a moment. 'But it'll keep.' He opened her door and she tried to move but her limbs had stiffened from her fall and he lifted her down, holding her against his chest as her legs buckled. 'Safer to leave it at coffee. Breakfast could so easily become habit-forming.'

'It won't,' she said, with a fierceness she hoped sounded convincing. She had come as close to that danger tonight as she was ever likely to. Despite the desperate yearning for him, as potent now as when his lips had first claimed hers, from somewhere she had found the strength to reject him. Not because she wanted to, but because she had to. They had wasted their chance at love and she wouldn't take whatever second-best he had in mind.

It was light when Clay finally turned the van into Mrs Grant's drive. She was at the door as they climbed down and hurried out as she saw them.

'Jo! I've been worried sick.' Her eyes fell on Clay and her worst fears were apparently confirmed.

'We broke down, Mum. We're all right. If I had thought you would be worrying I would have phoned. But I didn't think you would welcome a call in the middle of the night.'

'It was when I heard the forecast on the television. I telephoned Mrs Rhys and she told me you'd left hours before.'

'We . . .' Her mother's words sank in. 'Telephoned Mrs Rhys? But her phone was . . .' She turned on Clay, who regarded her without a flicker of expression, except, she thought, for something in his eyes that might have been amusement at how easy she had been to fool. Disconcerted, she looked away.

'Come along in, both of you. You look frozen.'

'I'll unload the van and get away, Mrs Grant,' he said, stiffly.

One look at his gaunt white face, shadowed where he needed to shave, and she softened despite herself. 'No. Come in by the fire. This will wait. Have you had breakfast?'

He glanced at Jo. 'I thought we'd better get back. I guessed you would worry.' Jo stifled the words that leapt to her lips and he raised one brow in mocking salute to her self-control. It would keep, she thought, following her mother into the house, but vowed that he would have a full account of her feelings on the matter when she felt stronger.

'Sit there, Clay.' Mrs Grant left him in an armchair by the fire and turned on Jo. 'You'd better get into a hot bath, right now.'

'Mum — '

'Later. She pushed Jo towards the stairs and she dragged herself up and stood for a while under a hot shower, afraid that she would fall asleep in a bath. She dressed in soft grey cord trousers and a yellow sweatshirt and went to look in on her daughter. Alys wasn't in her room and in a sudden panic she ran down the stairs.

'Where's — ?'

'Shh.' Her mother placed a finger to her lips and indicated Clay, slumped fast asleep in the armchair. 'I just rescued his cup in time. Come into the kitchen and have something to eat.'

Alys was already there, munching happily on a toast soldier that she offered to her mother. 'Mummy!'

'Hello, my sweet. Have you been a good girl?' It was easier to chatter to the child than meet her mother's knowing eye, but eventually she would have to be faced and the sooner the better.

'I'm sorry you were worried, Mum. The van broke down up in the mountains and we had to wait hours for a tow-truck.'

'That's close enough to Clay's explanation,' her mother said. 'The only thing neither of you has explained, Jo, was how you came to be together in the first place.'

'He had to go to Brynglas to see the site.'

'And you invited him along with you?'

'No!'

Her mother raised an eyebrow. 'But he came anyway. Well, I did warn you.'

'Yes, Mum, you warned me. But you really don't have to worry.' She gazed at Alys. 'My emotions are quite under control.'

Her mother's eyes shifted to the doorway and she spun around. Clay was standing there, a dishevelled figure in the bright kitchen.

'I'd better go.' He turned to Jo. 'Can we unload now?'

'Jo and I can do that later,' Mrs Grant interjected. 'Jo will drive you home now. You look as if you might fall asleep at the wheel. She can bring the van back to the office tomorrow.'

He looked as if he would refuse and Jo, realising the truth in what her mother said, quickly intervened. 'Mother's right, Clay.'

For a moment he stared at her, then he shrugged. 'Who's arguing?'

She turned to give Alys to her mother, but Mrs Grant shook her head. 'I'm afraid you'll have to take her with you, Jo. I've an appointment with the hairdresser in twenty minutes.'

Jo stared at her mother. 'But — '

'If you'll excuse me.' She nodded. 'Goodbye, Clay.'

He offered a half-smile. 'Mrs Grant.'

Jo shrugged. 'Come on, Alys. Let's get your coat on.' She was conscious of Clay standing behind her as she pulled the bright jacket over the child's dungarees.

'She's very like you.'

'Yes,' Jo quickly agreed. 'Everyone says that.' Before she could react he had bent and picked Alys up, holding her at arm's length, staring at her closely. Alys closed her eyes and giggled delightedly, kicking her little legs.

'Is there nothing of her father in her?'

'A — a little.'

His mouth tightened. 'How little?' he demanded.

'If you knew — him, you would see.' She took Alys from him and hurried outside to her car and fastened her firmly into her car seat.

Clay climbed into the passenger seat and closed his eyes. He didn't open them again until she pulled up outside the cottage. She left the engine running and waited for him to get out. He didn't move.

'You're home, Clay.'

He turned and looked towards the cottage. 'Yes. So I am. Come on.' He opened the door.

'No.' His face was implacable and she looked quickly away. 'I don't think that's a good idea.'

'That wasn't a request, Jo.' He grimaced as he straightened. 'God, I'm stiff. Bring Alys, then you'll be quite safe. That was your mother's intention, I take it?'

Jo glanced back at her daughter and

frowned slightly. 'Maybe.' She certainly hadn't been going to the hairdresser. Clay opened her door and she climbed out, every bruised muscle shrieking from maltreatment.

As she followed him up the path a movement on the roof caught her eye. The doves were tumbling in their crazy, free-fall flight, just as they had been the very first time she had come here.

'Look, Alys!' she said. Clay stopped for a moment and watched them both and when Jo looked up she saw his forehead crease slightly, as if trying to remember something. It brought her back to earth with a sudden shock. 'What do you want, Clay?'

He dragged himself back from wherever his thoughts had taken him. 'Want?' he asked. Then, as if something had struck him as particularly amusing, he smiled. 'It's time for that breakfast you keep promising me. I'm starving.' He didn't wait for her answer, but turned and opened the door and disappeared inside.

She stood rigid with shock. How dared he? Well, he could whistle for his breakfast. 'Come on, Alys.' But as she turned the little girl slipped her hand and dived through the doorway. 'Alys!' She could hear the soft burble of laughter disappearing towards the drawing-room, and a sudden vision of a fine nineteenth-century porcelain figure of Napoleon on horseback that adorned the sofa-table sent Jo racing after the child.

She came to an abrupt halt in the doorway. The furniture was covered in dustsheets and there were no ornaments to be broken. She took her daughter's hand and walked slowly around the ground floor. The desk in the study was uncovered and had obviously been used recently, but the morning-room was sheeted and the curtains drawn against the light. The kitchen was clean, tidy enough, but didn't gleam the way it had under Mrs Johnson's lavish care.

The fridge revealed little more than a

few basic necessities and Jo took out a box of eggs. She had the oddest feeling as she opened the cupboards, knowing exactly where everything would be, that nothing had been touched since she left.

Upstairs she could hear the shower running and she quickly began the task of making scrambled eggs and toast. She put some coffee in the cafetière and set the kettle to boil. Alys had found a cupboard to her liking and had begun to empty it on the kitchen floor, heaping baking tins in an unsteady pile, but Jo had no time to stop her. She was desperate to have everything ready so that she could beat a hasty retreat the minute Clay appeared.

She wasn't sure when she realised the water had stopped running, but something made her turn, and he was standing in the doorway watching her. He was wearing only a short towelling robe and his hair was still wet. She watched in desperate fascination as a droplet of water ran the curve of a tight curl and hung shimmering before splashing on to his neck and running down into the folds of his robe. She quickly put the plate on the table and pressed down the cafetière.

'Won't you join me?'

'I — no.' She turned away and began to pick up the dishes that Alys was playing with, pushing them back into the cupboard.

'Leave it,' he commanded. 'Mrs Johnson will be in later. I expect she'll want to start from scratch.'

'It's been a long time since she was here.' She had to say something.

'It's been a long time since anyone was here. I haven't quite made up my mind whether to move back in or sell the place.'

The thought of anyone else living in their home tugged at her heart-strings, but she had to face reality.

'It's a shame to leave it empty. Where have you been living?'

'I took a service flat in town after you left.'

'I didn't leave. You threw me out.'

'You would have stayed?' His mouth curved in distaste. 'Should I be flattered?'

She didn't reply. There seemed nothing to say. 'We'll be going, then.'

'Sit down, Jo.'

'I don't think — '

'How fortunate for you. Get another cup and sit down. I want to ask you something.' She sank on to the seat opposite him and watched him eat the breakfast she had prepared.

'Well?'

'Can your mother cope with . . . ?' He indicated Alys. 'She seems to be a handful.'

'It's not ideal. But while I'm staying there I think she would be hurt if I found a childminder. Once I've moved out, then it will be different.'

'Moved out?' He looked up. 'You're looking for a place of your own?' A vein began to throb at his temple. 'Or perhaps you're not on your own?'

She felt the colour leave her face.

'I'm a big girl, Clay. It's a long time since I lived at home.'

'Living with your mother must be rather cramping.' She was too shaken to make any response and he shrugged and poured himself another cup of coffee. 'You made a valid point the other day about the need for a crèche. I've had Personnel run a check on numbers and I believe we should go ahead.'

'Why would you do that?' she asked, suspiciously. 'It was vetoed before.'

'You're a single parent,' he said, with careless insolence. 'Surely I don't need to spell out the benefits to you?'

'There's no such thing as a single parent, Clay,' she replied with chilling intensity. 'It takes two people to make a baby.'

'A fact I'm well aware of. But which two?' His voice was cutting. 'You were careful enough to see she wasn't mine.'

Alys looked up from the floor and Jo glared at Clay. 'This conversation is at an end,' she said, with quiet force.

'Not quite.' His eyes were glittering hard. 'I have to know if you loved him.'

'With all my heart, Clay. Until the day I die.' To be able to say the words was a kind of relief. He didn't know, would never know that she meant him. But she knew and rejoiced as she said it. Then she saw the ice in his eyes and the joy froze into a hard, painful knot where her heart was beating far too fast.

'So where is he now?' he demanded. She moved back under the naked savagery in his face, until the chair back stopped her. It seemed forever that they were locked into that look. He straightened abruptly and turned from her. 'What a waste,' he said, contemptuously. 'Will you use the crèche if I go ahead?'

She blinked, momentarily thrown by the sudden shift in subject. 'Of course. But I don't understand what you will get out of it.'

'A loyal workforce.' He leaned across and caught her hand. He frowned and

214

looked down, for a moment focusing on her wedding-ring. Then, his mouth a hard, thin line, he went on, 'Good engineers are hard to find. And we have an agreement. I wouldn't want you to have any excuse to say that you must stay at home to look after Alys.'

She jerked her hand away. 'I can't afford to stop work on a whim to look after my daughter.'

'No? Not even with the money from your shares?' he demanded and his cold eyes froze her to the chair.

'I need that to buy somewhere . . .' She stopped. She was saying far too much.

'Somewhere to live?' he finished thoughtfully. 'Your demand to buy them back was nothing but a bluff and I let you off the hook. How careless of me. It won't happen again.' He smiled quite suddenly. 'So you think the nursery is a good idea?'

'Long overdue,' she agreed, somewhat raggedly.

'Then consider it a fact. And just

think how grateful all the other mothers who work for me will be to you.'

'And fathers. On behalf of all your employees I thank you for your generosity.' From somewhere she found the strength to stand. 'Come along, Alys. Time to go home.'

For once the child responded immediately and Jo swept down the path and tucked her into her car seat. As she turned the key in the ignition she glanced back at the cottage, saw Clay drawing back the curtains to let in the light and wondered if he had made up his mind to stay or to sell.

She spent the rest of the day recovering from what her mother infuriatingly referred to as her 'night on a bare mountain' and by the following morning was almost able to ignore the colourful crop of bruises decorating various bits of her, thankfully on the less exposed parts of her anatomy.

Next day she arrived at the office to find herself a heroine. 'However did you persuade him?'

Jo shifted uncomfortably. 'Persuade who?' she asked, but she had a feeling that she already knew the answer to that question.

'Mr Thackeray, of course. He's going ahead with a crèche.' The receptionist, who had two small children, was desperately grateful. 'I heard him, Jo! He was standing right where you are now and he told Peter that you had convinced him that it was the right move to make.'

'Peter Lloyd?'

'Yes. He was absolutely livid!'

'I'll bet. He thinks all mothers should be at home puréeing carrots for their offspring,' she said, flippantly. But she wasn't feeling flippant. If Clay had stood and discussed the plans in Reception, it was because he wanted everybody to know what was going on. Jo shivered and wondered if she was catching a cold.

The day continued with a series of interruptions as she received calls of congratulation from members of staff.

By early afternoon it was clear that everyone in the building knew that a nursery was proposed and she was the person who had persuaded the new chairman to make this concession. At three o'clock she was summoned to Reception for a delivery and, curious, she hurried down.

The basket of red roses was ostentatious. More, she thought angrily, it was positively vulgar. More appropriate for a film-star's dressing-room. Jo turned over the card. Nothing discreet in an envelope. Just a scrawled message for anyone to read, and undoubtedly the receptionist already had done so.

'A night to remember,' it read. It was unsigned, but the bold, slashing handwriting was unmistakable. Jo flushed deeply to the roots of her hair. Well, now everyone would know how she had managed to 'persuade' Mr Thackeray that the company needed a crèche. Or they would think they did, which came to the same thing.

She plucked the card from the basket

and tore it in two and dropped it in the waste basket. Then she turned to walk away. 'Aren't you going to take the flowers, Jo?'

She stopped and tried on a smile for size. Surprisingly, her face didn't break. 'Why don't you keep them here to decorate the hall? I really don't have room for them upstairs.' After all, they were for public consumption. He might as well get his money's worth. And her reputation was a small enough price to pay. But there were no more interruptions, only curious glances.

At five, lost in concentration, hardly aware that everyone had suddenly found something important to do elsewhere, she looked up to find herself alone except for Clay, leaning nonchalantly in the doorway. She glanced around and offered him a rueful smile. 'You certainly know how to clear a room.'

'It takes years of practice.' He perched himself on the edge of her desk. 'You came to the office in the van.

May I offer you a lift home?'

'I'd love one.'

He had clearly expected a swift rebuff and his eyes narrowed. 'Would you?'

'Of course. I've no particular affection for public transport, and besides, I'd hate to spoil your fun. You'd better be waiting in the front entrance just after five-thirty. I'd be sorry if anyone missed us leaving together.' He bowed slightly and rose to leave. 'But there is a price.'

He paused, apparently amused. 'You're in no position to make demands, my dear.'

She ignored this. 'I can't quite decide. I was wondering whether I might begin to use my married name,' she murmured, and waited, but there was only the slightest tightening of his jaw to show that he had heard. 'It would reinstate my reputation very nicely, don't you think? Put a stop to a lot of vulgar gossip.' She didn't wait for a reply. 'Or — '

'Or?' he demanded.

'Or perhaps the crèche should

be . . . ' She hesitated, wondering just how far she could go.

'Get on with it!'

'Free?'

'Don't be ridiculous, Jo.' He turned to leave. 'I'll see you in reception at five-thirty.'

She picked up a telephone and punched in a number as he walked away. 'Personnel? This is Jo Grant. I have an amendment for your records — '

His hand cut off the call and she replaced the receiver and waited.

'You're bluffing, Jo.'

'Am I?'

'You wouldn't use my name when we lived together. You won't do it now.'

She swallowed. 'We all have to make sacrifices.'

His face darkened. 'I had planned to charge fifty per cent of cost. That's very reasonable.'

The phone rang and she placed her hand on the receiver. 'Ten per cent?' she offered.

'Forty?'

The phone rang again and she picked it up, holding her hand over the mouthpiece. 'Twenty?' she countered and answered her caller. 'Hello. Yes, we appear to have been cut off. As I was saying, I have a change for your records.'

'Twenty-five!'

She smiled faintly. 'I'll call you back,' she told the girl in Personnel, and glanced at her watch. 'Twenty-five per cent will do very nicely. I'll meet you downstairs in half an hour.' As he turned to leave she stopped him. 'Clay!'

'Yes?'

'Thanks for the flowers.'

He nodded. 'I'm glad you liked them. They were — ' he hesitated, as if searching for an appropriate word ' — rather expensive.'

'Worth every penny,' she assured him, although as every head turned to watch her progress through Reception at the end of the day she wasn't so sure.

Clay took his time about settling her in the Aston and she bore it with good grace; he had paid dearly for his fun. But when he pulled into the pub on the ringroad she protested.

'No. After-work drinks are strictly for the boys. I have to get home.'

'I had no intention of taking you for a drink. I just didn't want to sit outside your mother's house with her twitching at the curtains. Will you have dinner with me tonight?'

'I think you've had your way quite sufficiently for one day. Besides, I may not be able to get a babysitter.'

'I'm sure your mother would be happy to oblige. There's something I want to discuss with you. Or perhaps this time I shall be forced to call your bluff.'

She frowned slightly. 'My bluff?'

The headlights of a car illuminated his face. 'There's no way you'd start calling yourself Thackeray, my dear. Is there?' he demanded when she made no reply.

She pulled a face. 'After that horrible basket of roses it would serve you right.

And if I did, I'd hold you to your promise to put an announcement in every national newspaper.'

'My promise — ?'

'Had you forgotten? Pick me up at about eight. Or would you prefer to meet me somewhere and avoid my mother altogether?'

He smiled a little grimly and reached for the ignition. 'I'll pick you up.'

8

Mrs Grant was not amused. She had been willing enough to babysit, but when Jo explained why she set her mouth in a grim little line.

'You're mad to go,' she said. 'He'll have you eating out of his hand again.'

Jo shook her head. 'No, I don't think so. He said he wants to talk about something.' She began to pick up Alys's toys. 'I think something I said today . . .' She clung to a teddy. 'I think he's going to suggest a divorce.'

'Oh.' Her mother took the toys from her. 'That would be a relief. But you'd better go and get ready. In the circumstances you'll want to look your best.'

Did she? She flipped idly through her clothes, wondering just what she could wear that would cover such a situation. She would never have sought a divorce because she would never love anyone else but Clay. But perhaps her mother was right. It would be for the best to cut the invisible ties that held them in thrall, no matter how painful the final severance would be. And there was no doubt that it would be painful. Despite everything, when he was in the room it was as if the lights had been switched on. Harsh light it might be, illuminating all too clearly every crack in their relationship. But for the first time since he had walked out of her life Jo felt alive. And that was dangerous.

She pulled out the dress she had bought for Redmonds' last Christmas dinner. She hadn't gone in the end because Alys had been unwell and there had been no reason since to wear it. Plain black. It seemed somehow appropriate.

She put Alys to bed and they played for a little while, then, when she couldn't put it off any longer, she went to get ready and in the process discovered that her mother was right. It was important that she look her very best.

She took extra care with her make-up, sprayed herself with an exotic scent her sister had bought for her birthday and fluffed her normally sleek hair into something altogether wilder. The dress, a slender tube of black crêpe, slipped smoothly over her hips, stopping just short of her feet, the hem dividing at the side in a graceful curve to display her ankle as she moved.

She fastened long plain gold drops to her ears, but wore nothing around her neck. The drama of the dress, black against the whiteness of her skin as it curved over one shoulder, leaving the other bare, needed no embellishment. Jo turned to examine her rear view in the mirror and wondered, briefly, how her bare arm and shoulder had so miraculously escaped bruising, when the other was a kaleidoscope of colour.

A brisk ring on the doorbell put an abrupt stop to her musings. She hadn't heard the Aston's throaty warning of his arrival. She threw a brief backward glance at her reflection, then hurried downstairs before her mother could say anything that everyone might regret. She caught her breath as she paused in the entrance to the drawing-room. Clay stood, his head bent slightly as he listened to something her mother was saying, his broad black-clad figure graceful, relaxed, certain of his power to charm. He turned and straightened as she moved towards them and as his eyes widened she was glad that she had taken so much trouble over her appearance.

'Joanna . . . ' He reached for her hands and she allowed her fingers to rest in his for the briefest moment. Longer would be too hard.

'Good evening, Clay,' she said, with a coolness that belied the way the blood was racing around her body. 'Has Mum offered you a drink?'

'She did, but I have explained that our table is booked for eight-thirty. We should go now.'

She acquiesced with a graceful nod.

'Where are we going?'

'I've planned a small surprise.'

She smiled slightly. 'Then I'll wait in the hall while you tell my mother where she can reach us in case she needs to get in touch.' A frown creased his forehead. 'Because of Alys,' she explained, and turned quickly away, wrapping herself in a cashmere shawl to disguise the fact that she was shaking with the effort of maintaining a cool poise, of keeping all her feelings firmly under lock and key.

He joined her moments later and his hand at her elbow led her firmly to a waiting taxi. 'The last time I felt like that I was seventeen years old.'

'Really?' she said. 'In what way?'

'Having to report where I was taking you to your mother!'

She stifled a giggle. 'Did she remind you to have me home before midnight?'

He glanced across at her. 'Not in so many words, Cinderella. I think she remembered, just in time, that I'm your husband.' Any desire to laugh deserted her. Apparently satisfied, he went on. 'I never could understand why parents believe that their daughter's virtue is safe until midnight. A triumph of hope over memory, perhaps?' he suggested.

'I'll bear that in mind when boys come calling for Alys.'

He stared at her. 'It's the boys who come calling for you that concern me.'

'If this is the kind of discussion you had in mind it is already at an end. You can take me home right now.'

'Too late.' The taxi pulled up. 'We've arrived.'

Jo looked out of the window and caught a glimpse of lights on the river. And with a sickening lurch of her heart she saw where he had brought her — to the same beautiful restaurant where they had come on that first night. She would never have believed that he could be so cruel.

He held out his hand and she dismissed the idea of refusing to get out of the taxi, demanding that he take her home. There was a challenge in his eyes, a dare. She lifted her chin, placed her hand in his and allowed him to lead her inside.

It hadn't changed. The low ceiling, the soft lighting and candles on the table invited lovers. The last time they had crossed this restaurant floor, happiness had lifted her; she had floated at his side and people had turned to watch them. Now pride kept her back ramrod-straight, kept the smile pinned to her mouth, and still people raised their heads and followed them with their eyes.

At last they were settled in a quiet corner, vast menus before them, and Jo sipped at a glass of champagne to moisten her dry mouth.

'Have you decided?'

'What?' She glanced down. 'Oh, no.' She stared at the jumble of words, unable to make them out. 'I'm not very hungry.'

'Shall I choose something for you?'

She nodded miserably. 'If we must eat.'

'I rather think it's expected.' His look brought the instant attention of the waiter and he ordered for them both, then refilled her glass.

They sat for a moment in silence. 'How is your father?' Jo asked, politely.

'His health isn't so wonderful, but he tries to keep active.'

'He sent me a card. At Christmas,' she explained. 'And a present, for Alys.'

'Rather more than he sent me. But then he believes I've robbed him of his grandchild.'

'I'm sure you've done your best to correct that impression.'

'I'm afraid not.' His eyes locked on hers. 'I preferred to cling to the remnants of my pride.'

Her hand shook and she put the glass down quickly. 'So that's why he wanted to see her? He believes she's yours . . . '

'It would make him very happy. He's not been too well. Could you bear it?'

'I tried to telephone him, but by the time his card had been sent on to Wales he had gone abroad.'

'He's back now.'

Jo didn't know what to say. Clay appeared to be inviting her to perpetuate what he believed to be a lie. It seemed oddly unlike him.

She was glad of the interruption of the waiter bringing them food. She stared at it for a moment and then picked up her fork and began to push the curls of smoked salmon about her plate.

'You really aren't hungry?' he asked.

She shook her head. Her stomach was tied in knots. 'You brought me here to discuss . . . something.'

'We've all evening.'

'I'd rather get it over with, if you don't mind.'

'I thought we might . . . ' He stopped. 'This was clearly a mistake, but we can hardly walk out in the middle of a meal.'

'For goodness' sake, Clay. I'm not stupid. I know what you want!'

He put the glass down on the table and looked at her. 'Do you?' He picked up her left hand. 'I rather doubt it. Tell me, why do you still wear your wedding-ring, Joanna? You left your diamond behind, but surely this was the important one?'

'The diamond had an intrinsic worth. This only has a value to me.' She made herself look up. 'Do you want it back?' she demanded.

A flush darkened his cheekbones. 'No, I do not!' His mouth tightened. 'And if it lends you a certain respect-ability I don't begrudge — '

She erupted from her chair. 'If I had wanted that kind of respectability, Clayton Thackeray,' she said, not caring who turned to stare at her, 'I could have used my married name any time I wanted.' She wrenched at the ring but it wouldn't come off. 'Damn! It always was too tight. I'll send it to you. By registered post!' She snatched up her bag and ran from the restaurant, pushing past people arriving, too much in distress to care.

A taxi was dropping someone and

she leapt in and gave her address. The driver picked up his radio to inform his office.

'Please hurry,' she urged him. But she was too late. The door opened and Clay slid in beside her. The driver turned and eyed them both. 'Same address, madam?'

'Yes, please.'

'But take the scenic route.'

The driver regarded Clay evenly. 'It's the lady's cab, sir.'

Suddenly ashamed of her loss of control, she raised her hand hopelessly. 'It's all right.' They had to talk, and the sooner it was over the better. She shivered.

'You're cold. Here.' He slipped his jacket around her and somehow his arm stayed there, wrapping her in his strength. Just now she needed all the strength in the world.

'I shouldn't have made a scene,' she apologised stiffly. 'I didn't mean to.'

'I found the crack in the self-control . . . illuminating.'

'I'm glad it served some purpose. But it was the last time. You can have your divorce.'

He swung to face her, a deep frown creasing his forehead. 'Is that what you want?'

'It's for the best.' She looked away, disconcerted by the intensity of his gaze. 'But I think that in the circumstances I really would like to look for another job. Will you let me go? Please, Clay?'

There was a muscle working at the corner of his mouth. 'I can't hold you beyond the three months' notice you're obliged to give.'

The chill flooded back as he removed the comfort of his arm. Three months! Her insides caved in at the thought. It was less than three weeks and already she was at the edge of her endurance. 'Surely you wouldn't force me to continue working for you in the circumstances?'

'I'm letting you off lightly. Three months. I'll expect to hear from your solicitors.' He tapped on the glass. 'Stop here.' The driver pulled up and Clay passed him some notes and climbed out. 'Please take my wife wherever she wants to go.'

'Clay! You can't get out here!' The mist was swirling along the river. 'At least take your jacket!' She held it out of the window but he didn't turn back. 'Idiot!' She opened the door and began to run after him. 'Clay!' He'd disappeared from the road and she swung about her, trying to see where he had gone. Then she realised where she was. After a moment's hesitation she plunged down the towpath, cursing furiously as she stepped in a puddle, slithering on the damp mud in her high heels. 'Clay!' she screamed after him. Something rustled in the bushes beside her and she spun around. There was something there; she couldn't see what. Then it moved again and she took off in panic, desperate to get away from the heavy breathing close at her heels. 'Clay!' she shouted hoarsely, and was brought to an abrupt halt as something grabbed her. She tried to scream, but the terror closed her throat and turned her tongue to wood.

'What the hell do you think you're doing?'

It was him. She saw him as he spun her round and in her relief she threw herself at him, clinging to him while she tried to catch her breath. 'There . . . was . . . something . . . ' Braver in his arms, she turned to confront her pursuer. A large black and white dog was sitting on the path, head expectantly on one side. 'Oh!' she gasped, feeling suddenly very foolish. She slumped against him as relief washed over her. 'It was a dog.'

'What did you think it was?' His voice was chilly, shocking sense back into her. She managed to let go and step back.

'You . . . ' she held up his jacket ' . . . left this.' He didn't take it and she let her hand fall. 'I thought you'd be cold.' She shivered, and with a muffled exclamation he took the jacket and draped it around her shoulders.

'Whatever am I going to do with you now?' he demanded.

'Do with me?' She stiffened. 'Do with me?' She stifled a sob. 'Please don't trouble yourself on my account!' She turned and began to walk quickly back the way she had come.

'Trouble?' he yelled after her. She faltered, but stumbled on. 'You've been nothing but trouble since the day I set eyes on you.' She forced herself to keep walking but he caught her arm and swung her round to face him. 'Stop, damn you!'

'Why?' she demanded. 'If I'm so much trouble you should be glad to see the back of me.'

'I know that. I thought I would be. But it didn't work, so I took my chance when Charles died and took control of Redmonds. I wanted to make you watch as I took it to bits. Then I could clear you out of my mind along with the debris. It was the only way I could think of to hurt you the way you hurt me.'

'But . . . you're expanding, opening a nursery. Oh, God!' With sudden clarity she saw it all. 'It's just a cruel hoax, and when they find out they'll crucify me. I'll never get another job — '

'That was the general idea — '

'And the breakdown?' she demanded bitterly. 'Was that all part of the plan?'

'No. The accident was genuine enough.' He paused, then added, 'But another mile and we would have run out of petrol.'

'So why didn't you see it through?' she demanded, furiously. 'Surely it was a little squeamish to stop at rape?'

'You wouldn't understand,' he said fiercely. 'Not in a million years.' He turned and began to walk away from her.

She followed, suddenly desperate. 'You can't do it, Clay. I'm not asking for myself. I don't matter. Please . . . I'll do anything you want.'

'Anything?' He paused and his look was cynical. 'You haven't changed, then. I thought . . . ' He threw back his head and groaned. 'God help me, I thought — '

She snapped. 'Thought?' she demanded wildly. 'When did you ever stop to think?' She felt all control slipping away as she flung an angry fist at his shoulder, rocking him back on his feet.

He turned four-square to her, offering himself as a target. 'Yes! Come on, Jo, let it out. You're so bottled up that it's a wonder you don't explode with all that suppressed emotion. I've goaded you, taunted you, embarrassed you beyond endurance and you just take it. What will it take to make you let go? What are you so afraid of?'

'I'm not afraid!' she yelled.

'No? Prove it. Come on. Why have you chased down the towpath after me? Can't you admit the truth to yourself?'

'Truth? What truth?'

'This. The only truth there ever can be between a man and a woman.' He jerked her roughly against him.

'No! Clay!' As she realised his intention she began to struggle.

'Too late, my darling. You said anything. I'm taking you at your word.' His mouth claimed hers with absolute conviction and after the first momentary shock-wave, when she could neither move nor think, she found herself clinging to him, responding with a burning urgency that met him head-on.

When, finally, the need to catch breath drove them apart, they stood, their breasts heaving, staring at one another in astonishment. Then she reached for him, lost beyond any sense of danger.

'Not here,' he said hoarsely and grabbed her hand. They ran wildly along the path, carelessly splashing through the muddy puddles, heedless of the curls of mist drifting along the water or a distant church clock proclaiming the hour.

He looped his arm around her waist as he searched for the key to the cottage door, and they almost fell inside as it suddenly gave way under their combined weight.

Once inside, he gathered her once more in his arms, kissing her like a man starved, and Jo wasn't listening to the warning voice of common sense screaming in her ears. She was suffering from a kind of madness, a long-suppressed hunger for him, and she was no longer capable of stopping what was now inevitable even if she had wanted to.

With a fierce, hungering cry he seized her in his arms and carried her up the stairs and over the threshold into what once, aeons ago, had been their bedroom.

She lay back against his chest, revelling in the sight of his body outlined by the damp cloth of his shirt as it clung to his shoulders, and of his thick dark mat of curls decorated with a film of mist.

She wrapped her arms around his neck and slid to her feet, moulding herself against him. Then she began to undo his shirt-studs, frowning in concentration.

'Joanna . . . ' Her name was wrung from him.

She raised her wide grey eyes to his. 'I'm reacting, Clay. Letting go. It's been a long time and I'm not sure I remember how. Help me.'

His hands seized her zip and tugged it and with a soft sigh she shrugged out of her dress, leaving it to ripple to the floor.

He dragged her to him. 'God help me, I can't resist you.' He tilted her face to his and kissed her, a long, possessive kiss that set her aflame. Then they were shedding their clothes and she gasped as he reached for her once more and held her hard against him. 'Is that what you want, Joanna?' he asked, roughly.

Her legs were too weak to hold her and she clung to him. 'Yes,' she whispered.

'You're sure it's me you want?' he grated.

'There's never been anyone else . . . ' She moved urgently against him and with a primitive roar he bore her to the bed, smothering her with wild kisses that covered her eyes, her chin, her throat until every last vestige of her hard-won control was shattered and she was shouting, screaming at him, demanding that he take her.

He raised his head and for a moment held her, pinned by his body to the bed, taking in her dark, passion-soaked eyes and her heaving breast. Then, with a smile of triumph, he rolled away on to his back.

'Make me,' he invited.

There was a wildness in her that blotted out everything but the two of them. With a delighted laugh she accepted his invitation, reaching for him, trailing her fingers through the tight curls of his chest until a fingertip brushed the tiny bud of his nipple and she heard the sharp intake of his breath. She moved over him, caressing him with her breasts, outlining his lips with her tongue, tasting the salt of his skin.

He moved then, to take her, but she stopped him, holding him in suspense for one long moment until, very slowly, she lowered herself on to him.

For the space of a heartbeat nothing happened. Then he seized her and rolled over, until she in turn was the one who was dominated and she was plummeting in crazy, giddy waves of sensation that swept her to a wild culmination before he surrendered to his own convulsive release. They clung together until the shock-waves passed and at last they were still, entwined in each other's arms.

She must have slept briefly, because when she opened her eyes Clay was standing over her, dressed in a dark tracksuit.

'I've dried your clothes as best I can.'

She clutched the covers around her. 'What time is it?'

'It's after one.'

'So late!'

He nodded. 'I'll bring the car round to the front.'

Thankful for the privacy, she quickly dressed and straightened her hair as best she could, but her reflection in the mirror was brutally honest. To anyone with half an eye to see, it was obvious what she had been doing. She stopped the thought. There would be time enough to worry about that later.

He drove swiftly through the quiet streets, concentrating wholly on the mechanics of driving, leaving her to her thoughts. He stopped the car in the road outside her mother's home, opened the door for her and walked her up the drive.

'Clay — '

'Tomorrow, Joanna. Now is not the time to talk.' He took her key and slid it silently into the lock and pushed the door open. 'I'll come round about eleven.'

'Tonight was just a madness, Clay. I want you to forget that it ever happened. Promise me.'

'Tomorrow,' he said abruptly. 'We'll talk tomorrow. Please, go in.'

'Jo?' Her mother's voice floated down the stairs. 'Is that you?'

'Send her my apologies,' Clay murmured. 'Tell her the pumpkin broke down.' He dropped a kiss on her cheek. 'Goodnight.'

She watched him until he ducked into the car. He raised a hand in salute and then slid silently away from the kerb.

'Jo?' Her mother appeared at the bottom of the stairs clad in a woollen dressing-gown.

'It's me, Mum. Sorry I'm so late.'

'No problem. Alys never murmured.' Her mother regarded her thoughtfully for a moment. 'Well? Were you right? Did he ask you for a divorce?'

'I believe we've settled all the outstanding issues,' she said with a gallows smile. 'He's coming round in the morning to discuss the details.'

'Didn't you have enough time tonight?' her mother asked innocently. She didn't wait for an answer but wandered into the kitchen and put on the kettle. 'Tea?' she offered.

'I'll go straight to bed if you don't

248

mind. It's been quite a week, one way and another.' Not that she would sleep. What remained of the night would have to be spent putting her shattered self-control back together. She just hoped she could find all the pieces.

* * *

Alys woke her mother with joyful quacking. 'Ducks! Feed the ducks!' she shouted, and started to quack again.

Joanna lay still for a moment, her limbs oddly leaden, and tried to recall when she had last felt those familiar aches. She hauled herself up and looked at the clock. It was ten-thirty. She frowned for a moment, knowing that there was something important she should remember. Then it all came flooding back. She leapt out of bed and, shutting the door so that Alys couldn't escape, dived under the shower.

The steaming water breathed some life back into her and she dressed simply in a pair of jeans and a soft shirt.

'Mum!' She picked Alys up and carried her down the stairs. 'Mum?'

'In here, dear.'

She followed her mother's voice into the living-room and found her sitting before the fire, talking to Clay, who rose at her entrance.

'Hello, Joanna.'

She paled and had to swallow before the words would come. 'Hello, Clay.'

She knew she was blushing like a fifteen-year-old. Her mother looked from Joanna to Clay, and back again. 'Clay brought you some roses, Jo. They're in the kitchen.'

'Roses?' She made herself smile. 'Not red ones, I hope?'

'Pink seemed safer,' he said evenly.

Alys wriggled free of her mother's grasp and ran to her grandmother. 'Feed ducks,' she said.

'I'm sorry, sweetheart, not today.' The older woman looked up. 'I promised her a trip down to the river this morning. I hate to disappoint her, but I've a slight headache.' She touched her brow delicately.

'I'll take her later,' Jo promised.

'Why wait?' Clay stood up. 'We'll go now.'

'Well, how kind. She's all ready and there's a bag of bread in the kitchen.'

Jo looked from her mother to Alys, who was dressed in her bright blue dungarees that so perfectly echoed her eyes. She wasn't sure what game her mother was playing but she wasn't about to become one of the pawns.

'No, Mum. Not if you're not well.'

'I'm sure your mother would prefer us to take Alys out of her way, Joanna. Get your coat on.'

'But I haven't had any breakfast!'

'It's far too late for breakfast. I'll buy you a cup of tea at the hut in the park,' he offered.

'However could I refuse an offer like that?' she said, furious at the way she was being manipulated. But she went off to dress Alys in her outdoor clothes and then fastened her into her pushchair.

Clay lifted her out of the door and before she could take over had set off down the road. She called goodbye to her mother and raced after him.

'I'll push,' she said.

'I think I can manage. It's not that difficult.' He looked down at her. 'If you were to link your arm through mine we would look like any ordinary married couple.'

'But we're not.'

'Humour me.' He offered her his elbow. She hesitated, knowing only too well how her body reacted to his touch. Aware of her reluctance, he paused. 'I'm not likely to eat you in the street,' he said. With the utmost reluctance she slid her arm through the crook of his arm and he clamped it firmly to his side, giving her no opportunity to change her mind.

He halted at a crossing and waited for the cars to stop. Alys looked up at him.

'Ducks?' she asked, hopefully.

'Soon, sweetheart.' He laughed and

turned to Jo. 'She has a recognisable single-mindedness.'

'Yes, I'm afraid so. Clay — '

'We can cross now.'

They walked beside the river in silence, Clay concentrating intently on negotiating the pushchair through the people brought out by the winter sunshine, Jo trying very hard to remind herself that this interlude had nothing to do with the reality of their lives.

They crossed the stone bridge over the entrance to the lock and on to the island where the ducks were greedily waiting for early visitors. She watched helplessly as Clay released Alys and lifted her from the chair, carrying her close enough to feed them.

It all had such a heartbreaking normality. She had rejected all this because she had been hell-bent on a career. Hell-bent on proving to her father — proving to herself — that she was as good as the son he had been denied by her own birth. Now, standing watching Clay and Alys, she realised the

253

sum of what she had lost.

He turned to her and held out the bag of bread. 'Come on.' She joined the two of them in their game reluctantly, not because she didn't want to be part of the charmed circle, but because afterwards, when it was over, the pain would be total.

For a while they watched the little girl toddling about among the birds, chasing them and being chased, Clay guarding her path to the water, taking care that the ducks didn't get too close to her little fingers. Finally, the bread all gone, he picked her up and swung her on to his shoulders. 'Right, young lady. It's time your mother had her tea.'

He gave her no opportunity to object, but strode purposefully back the way they had come, leaving Jo to follow with the buggy. By the time she caught them up they were already inside the cosy park hut, choosing from a display of home-made cakes.

'Can she have one of those?' Clay asked, as Alys pointed to an éclair.

Jo shook her head. 'No. She can have some toast.'

'Spoilsport. What about you?'

'I'll have a slice, too.'

They sat at the table, Alys perched on Clay's knee. He loosened her jacket, fielding her neatly as she made a dive for the salt-pot. 'Oh, no, you don't, miss.' Alys smiled winningly, then turned her attention to the zip on his pocket.

'Jo — ' He stopped as the woman brought tea and toast for them all. 'Thank you.' He began again. 'Jo, last night — '

'Last night was an aberration, Clay. It was the tension, the fight. You've no need to feel guilty.'

'I don't.' He frowned. 'I'm sorry that you feel it necessary to pull on a hair shirt.'

'I shouldn't have let it happen.'

'But it did. It was inevitable from the moment you followed me. You must have known that.'

'No!' She saw the woman behind the

counter peer in her direction and shook her head, lowering her voice. 'No. It was just madness — '

'Jo,' he interrupted, 'I want you to come back to me.'

9

Joanna felt the blood drain from her face. 'Come back to you?' She shook her head in an effort to clear the hammering from her ears.

He reached across the table and grasped her hand. 'I know you asked me for a divorce, Jo, but think about it.' His eyes blazed at her. 'Think about last night.'

She refused to let her mind draw out the pictures of that fierce passion. He had married her for that, had made no secret of it. It hadn't been enough then. How could it be enough now, with all that had happened a thorny barrier between them? She snatched her hand from his warm grasp. Even the touch of his fingers was enough to weaken her resolve.

'No,' she said, quickly, before the temptation overwhelmed her. 'It's not possible.'

The blue eyes suddenly chilled. 'There's someone else?' She shook her head vehemently. 'What other reason could there be?' he persisted.

'I should have thought that was obvious,' she said, her eyes automatically straying to her daughter.

He glanced down at Alys, perched on his knee, contently chewing on a piece of toast. 'She's beautiful, Jo. Like her mother. If she had been . . . different — '

'Like her father?' she offered, glad of the sudden chill that drove the weakness from her heart.

He looked up. 'I'd treat her as if she were my own.'

She sat back, suddenly exhausted by the emotional drain of it all. As if she were his own. The words mocked her. Even with the child in front of him, he couldn't see it. She is yours . . . She rehearsed the simple phrase in her head, but never spoke the words. He would never believe it, no matter how much she protested.

'Please, Clay. Don't go on with this.'

But he persisted. 'What happened was an aberration; I was stupid to have left you on your own.' Once more he fielded her hand as if he knew instinctively that his touch had the power to persuade her. 'I won't, ever again.' There was a fierce implacability about his mouth that gave her the strength to deny him.

'Surely, Clay, that's the point? You'd never trust me out of your sight. I'm sure the cage would be comfortable,' she tried to make him see, 'but it would still be a cage, with you constantly on your guard every time another man came too close, in case I felt like breaking out.'

'No,' he swore. And yet the whiteness around his mouth told her it was the truth.

For a moment she considered trying to convince him that she had never looked at another man since he'd come into her life. Had never wanted to. But he wouldn't believe her. Perhaps he couldn't. And it would destroy her utterly to see the disbelief in his eyes.

'A relationship needs trust, Clay. Neither of us quite succeeded in establishing that. We didn't know each other well enough to marry. It was my fault. I allowed you to overwhelm me because, heaven knows, I wanted to be overwhelmed. But it was too soon. You should have been content with an affair. Although I suspect you had your own reasons for preferring the commitment of marriage.'

'That's not true!'

'You expect me to believe you when you refused to listen to me?'

He was silent for a moment, then his mouth twisted into a self-mocking little smile. 'An impasse.' He lifted Alys down. 'I think we'd better go.'

For a moment she didn't move. An almost unbearable sadness weighed so heavily at her limbs that the effort of standing seemed too much. Clay's hand at her elbow galvanised her into movement and she bent to take Alys by the hand, automatically returning the smiles of two elderly ladies who stood aside in the doorway to let them out.

'What a lovely child,' the first one said, and turned back to her friend. 'Isn't she lovely, Molly? And so like her mother.'

Alys, always delighted with attention, smiled expectantly at Molly.

The old lady reached out and touched the mop of fair hair and looked up at the tall figures of Joanna and Clay.

'Charming. And as you say, dear, she is like her mother.' Then she smiled at Clay. 'But she has your eyes. Quite unmistakable.'

Slowly — almost, Jo thought, in slow motion — he bent and swung Alys up, holding her out in front of him, looking at her as if he had never seen her before. Alys stared solemnly back at her father, then raised her chubby hands to his face. With a sigh he drew her close and folded her tenderly in his arms. Then, without a word, he walked from the hut, striding purposefully away, leaving Jo to hurry after him.

'Clay, wait,' she said, but he took no notice and, hampered by the pushchair, she was forced into a ridiculous half-run in an effort to keep pace with him.

He forged ahead and her heart gave an enormous sigh of relief when he turned into the driveway instead of bundling the child into the Aston and spiriting her away. But her relief was short-lived as he turned to her, hand outstretched.

'Your car keys,' he demanded. Faced with a white-faced man holding her child, she handed them over without hesitation. He unlocked the door. 'Get in.'

'Alys — '

'Leave Alys to me.' She watched as he fastened her securely into the car seat. 'Get in, Jo,' he repeated, quite unnecessarily. She wasn't going to let Alys out of her sight. She slid quickly into the passenger seat and fastened her seatbelt.

He climbed in beside her and carefully backed out of the drive. Then, as if driving on eggs, his concentration total, he drove three silent miles to Redmonds' office. Without speaking, he unfastened Alys and carried her inside.

'What are you doing, Clay?' Jo demanded. 'Why have you come here?'

He glanced at her coldly, not bothering to answer, before turning in the direction of the basement. She was pulled after him by his possession of her daughter, following him down the stairs to the room where the records for all the jobs that Redmonds had ever undertaken were stored. He flicked the bank of switches, flooding the huge area with light, then set off purposefully along the racks of plans and box files, his eyes narrowed, searching.

'What do you want?' she asked, in a sort of desperation. 'Perhaps I can help you find it?'

'Really?' His voice was chilling.

After that she said nothing, merely following him. Alys had fallen asleep across his shoulder, perfectly content, but Jo never let them out of her sight for a moment.

Finally, with a exclamation of satisfaction, he pulled a file from the shelf. He laid it gently on the table, so as not to disturb the sleeping child, and began to turn the pages.

Jo frowned. They were pink timesheets for the bridge job she had been working on when she met Clay. He leafed through them quickly until he found the day he was looking for and she saw him blench as he flicked through each one, signed by her.

'You worked that night.'

So that was what he was looking for. Proof.

'I told you I did.'

He turned then to face her. 'Could I have been that wrong? Lloyd . . . '

'Peter brought me home because he thought I was too tired to drive and if I had had an accident he would have had to explain why I was working while he was off at a family party. No other reason. He wouldn't give me the time of day unless I paid him for it.'

He frowned. 'But you . . . he kissed you. And before. I saw you kissing him before.'

'Yes, Clay. You saw me kissing him.' She shuddered at the thought. 'After you had rejected me. I'd offered you myself without any strings because I had fallen hopelessly, totally in love. At least I thought it was love.' She forced a careless shrug. 'At least you corrected that childish fantasy.'

'Then why — ?' He grabbed at her shoulder and Alys stirred. With a smothered oath he released Jo and, as if he had been doing it all his life, gently settled Alys back to sleep. 'Why did you kiss him?' he demanded, his voice quiet but the soft tone as dangerous as ever.

'Because you were there, standing in the doorway of the pub, completely mis-understanding what you were seeing; I was angry. Very angry.' She refused to meet his eye. 'I did it without thinking, to make you jealous. I knew I'd have to pay for it. I just hadn't realised how much.' She made a dismissive gesture. 'Peter Lloyd isn't a very pleasant man. I was half-asleep when he kissed me that time he brought me home, or he would never have got so close.'

Clay uttered a soft groan of pain. 'There never was anyone else.' It wasn't a question, but she answered him anyway.

'No, Clay, there was never anyone else.'

He touched the sleeping child's head. 'She's mine? She's really mine?'

Jo nodded. 'After you left for Canada I did some thinking. I realised how wrong I'd been. I hadn't considered your feelings at all. I'd excluded you. I . . . I had my own reasons for not wanting a family so soon.'

'Your career.' He bit the words off as if they were something dirty.

She nodded unhappily. 'If you like.' She looked up at him desperately. 'But I threw the rest of the pills away. I thought that when you came home from Canada we could sit down and talk it through. Make some decisions together.' She pulled a face. 'Apparently I did the worst possible thing.' Then she touched the sleeping child. 'Except that it was the right thing. The best thing I ever did.'

'Now you must come back.'

She took a deep breath. 'Because you have your proof? I don't think so, Clay. It's too late for us. You've found your daughter; be content.'

He looked for a moment as if he would argue. Instead he nodded as if he understood how she felt. 'Will you let me see her?'

'Of course.'

He kissed the sleeping head. 'Come on, I'll take you both home.'

★ ★ ★

'Where is he taking her?' Her mother's lips were thin with disapproval.

Jo shrugged in an attempt to hide her nervousness. 'He said they might go to the zoo. Isn't that the classic Sunday haunt for all separated fathers?'

'That's too far!' she protested. 'He won't know what to do with her.'

'I pointed that out myself but he said he'd think of something. He's very resourceful. He'll cope.'

The sharp ring at the door plucked at her already shredded nerves, and the trembling about her midriff belied her casual acceptance of the possibility that he might have a woman in tow. To her relief he was alone.

'She's all ready.' Alys giggled with delight as Clay picked her up.

'Daddy!' she cried.

Jo had been coaching the little girl with this new word all week, but her timely use of it was totally unexpected. Clay's face whitened. When he had recovered he looked at Jo.

'Thank you.'

She managed a casual shrug. 'It's a new word. I warn you, she'll use it endlessly.'

'I shan't complain.' He picked up the

child's bag. 'Where's your coat?'

'Coat?'

'Yes, my dear, your coat.' He looked down at the bag he was holding. 'The contents of this are a complete mystery to me. I shall need walking through the details.'

'But you said you would manage,' she protested.

'So I will.' His smile was inviting. 'If you'll help?'

'And if I won't come?' she asked, suddenly certain that he had intended this from the first.

He looked into the drawing-room. 'I suppose I'd have to stay here all day. If your mother would put up with me,' he added, doubtfully.

'I'll get my coat.'

Alys was already tucked into her car seat when she emerged. Clay had asked to borrow her car for that very reason, offering to loan her the Aston in return. Now she wondered if it had simply been a ruse to ensure that she couldn't be out when he arrived.

They had been driving for a few minutes when Jo realised that he wasn't taking the road to London. 'I thought we were going to the zoo,' she said.

'It's too cold.'

'Alys is well wrapped up.'

'I know. But . . . ' he glanced across at her ' . . . it's my father's birthday. I promised him a special present. Is it a dreadful imposition?'

'You should have told me where you intended taking her,' she said, stiffly. 'I have a right to know. Suppose something happened?'

'But you're with us, so you do know.'

Jo went cold as she realised how easily he could have taken Alys and disappeared without trace and she might never have seen her daughter again. She had heard of such things happening.

'Don't play games with me, Clay. I bore Alys alone and raised her when you chose to think I was nothing but a — a — wanton.' She almost choked on the word. 'Suddenly I'm acceptable again because I have what you most want.'

With a low curse he pulled into the side of the road. 'It wasn't like that. I wanted you to come.' He reached out for her but she flinched away, refusing the easy comfort of his arms. He sat back, staring sightlessly out through the windscreen. 'I would have told you, but I didn't think you'd agree.'

'You thought right,' she said.

'Do you want me to take you home?'

For a moment she sat, her hands in tight fists, forcing herself to remember the pain of his rejection, his unwillingness to believe what she told him. But the face of Clay's father intruded, a gentle man who had been unfailingly kind to her. It wasn't his fault that his son's behaviour had deprived him of his grand-daughter's company. She breathed out very slowly and shook her head.

'No. We'll go on. But don't ever try something like this again.' She forced herself to look at him, to ignore the disconcerting hunger in his eyes. 'And, in the future, please make alternative arrangements for the care of Alys, because I shall not be available as a nanny.'

His mouth clamped together in a hard line. 'In that case I shall have to forgo the pleasure of my daughter's company.'

'No, that's silly. You could always find someone — '

'To take your place?' he offered. 'Do you think I would have come back if there had been the remotest possibility that I could ever love anyone else?'

'Love?' The word escaped her lips as, startled by the vehemence in his voice, she turned to him.

His lips curved in a self-mocking little smile. 'Silly, isn't it?' He slid the car into gear and, checking the road was clear, pulled out. Only Alys's occasional muttering broke the silence, mostly unintelligible. But once her high, clear voice called 'Daddy!' and they both visibly jumped.

The visit was not as awful as she'd

feared. Mr Thackeray was overjoyed with his granddaughter and the initial coolness between the two men soon thawed in their competition to amuse her. As they were leaving, Clay's father extracted a promise Jo gladly gave: to visit him often.

'Don't feel you must wait for Clay to bring you,' he told her when they were alone.

'I won't,' she promised.

'And if you need anything . . . ' He looked at her fiercely and she realised that he too had those blue eyes. Faded a little, but just as powerful. 'Anything at all,' he reiterated, 'come to me.' He raised his head to stare out of the window to where his son was packing the car. 'You don't have to go to Clay.'

'I never have.'

'No. Well, you're both strong characters. Differences were bound to arise, but I thought . . . ' He shrugged. 'His mother and I married within days of our first meeting, you know. I suppose I'm just a silly old man, but I thought you two had that same 'till death us do part' kind of love.'

'Sometimes that's not enough, Mr Thackeray.'

★　★　★

Clay carried in the bag and buggy when they got home and found her reading a note from her mother saying that she had gone to babysit for Heather.

'In that case,' Clay said, with satisfaction, 'I don't feel an urgent need to leave. Can I help you to bath Alys and put her to bed?'

'No.' The word came out too sharply and Jo was sorry for that as he almost flinched at her fierceness, but she was already stretched to breaking-point emotionally. 'It's been a tiring day. Alys has had quite enough excitement.'

'In that case I'll wait until you've finished. There's something I have to say to you, and unless you would rather I make an appointment at the office . . . ?'

'That won't be necessary. Help

yourself to a drink; I won't be long.'

Wearily Jo climbed the stairs, Alys a dead weight in her arms. She accomplished her daughter's bath with indecent haste, dressed her in a one-piece pyjama-suit and lifted her into her cot.

'Goodnight, Alys.' She kissed the child and tucked in her teddy-bear.

'Daddy?' she asked.

'Bedtime, Alys,' Jo warned.

Alys stuck out her lower lip. 'Daddy!' she said, raising her voice.

'Did someone call?'

She turned as Alys raised her hands. 'G'night, Daddy!'

He bent over the cot and stroked the fair hair. 'Goodnight, princess.'

Jo stumbled from the room and after a while Clay joined her in the living-room and poured himself another drink.

'You must come back, Jo.' His back was a wall between them.

'Because of Alys?'

'That's one reason. But only one.' He turned then. 'I was a fool. There. I've said it and I hope it gives you some satisfaction. I was jealous because I loved you beyond any reason and you refused to let me into your life.'

'Love?' That word again, and she wouldn't, mustn't allow it to influence her. 'Why do you persist in saying you loved me when we both know why you married me?'

'Do we?' He drained the glass. 'I'm beginning to wonder. If I had wanted your damned shares I could have had them for the asking.' His eyes challenged her. 'That's the truth, Joanna. Be honest with yourself.'

She flushed. It was the truth. He could have taken them from her and she would have begged him to do it.

'Yes,' she whispered. 'It's true.' She raised her lashes. 'So why didn't you?'

'Don't you know? Even now?' He was beside her in a stride. 'Because I loved you. I still love you.' He put his arms around her and held her gently. 'I didn't want to ask you to do anything that might spoil that.' Her sigh was a long, painful wrench from the heart. 'I wanted control of Redmonds — I admit it. More than that: I'll admit I was prepared to seduce them out of you.'

He refused to let her leave the circle of his arms. 'Be still and listen to me. It's time you heard it all.' She stood very still as he continued. 'I came looking for your father to enlist his aid. My solicitors had written to him, offering a good price for his shares, but he had turned it down. Except it wasn't your father I found. It was you. And an odd mixture of innocence and self-assurance you were. I'll confess I didn't know quite what to make of you. But when I trailed the offer of a flirtation you were quick enough to respond.'

She tried to speak then, but he stopped her, holding a finger to her lips. 'Not yet. I haven't finished, my love. I have to tell you that when you lay in my arms and told me you were a virgin I couldn't go ahead with it. Too cynical by half.' He smiled faintly. 'But it was too late, you see; I was bewitched. I was already far too deeply in love.'

She raised her face at last to his. 'But I was certain you married me to gain control of my shares. Not at first, but then there were rumours . . .'

'The shares had nothing to do with it. Unlike you, my darling Joanna, I was always able to keep my business and personal lives quite separate.' He swept her exclamation aside. 'If you had decided to sell I would have explained. But you were adamant that you had no intention of selling. Henry gained the same impression, and so long as you held your shares I could win.'

'I never meant to sell them. But Charles convinced me it was the right thing to do.'

'I believe you. He was lucky that I ended up with enough stock to fend off anyone else with similar ideas. Redmonds was a company begging to be taken over. An unwieldy management system that was totally out of control and an autocrat at the helm who wouldn't let go even when he was too sick to work.'

'And a big fat pension fund. Ripe for the plucking.'

'Exactly. Just what I didn't want to happen. Redmonds is too good a company to be destroyed that way.'

'You could have explained. All I heard were rumours. Then I discovered you knew Henry Doubleday and it was all too clear.'

'Why didn't you come to me?' he demanded.

She shook her head. 'When I first heard the rumours, first thought you might be involved, I didn't want to believe them. I didn't want to believe what that would mean. I wanted to trust you, believe you loved me. By the time I had proof it was too late.' She forced herself to look up into his face, search for any hint that he was lying. 'You said you bought the company to hurt me — '

'Maybe I did. God knows I tried to hurt you that night alone on the mountain when I had you completely at my mercy. It would have been so easy.

But I couldn't. Love was finally all I had.'

'Oh, Clay. I'm sorry. So very sorry. But I didn't know. You never told me.'

'It was careless of me. I assumed you realised. And I'm telling you now. I'll never allow you to forget if you'll give me a second chance to prove just how much I love you.'

She rested her cheek against his broad chest, feeling the steady comfort of his heartbeat. 'It's not just for Alys?'

He held her away from him, his eyes blazing with a powerful emotion that she couldn't begin to understand. 'If you tell me now that it's over, that there's no chance for us, I'll go away. The hurt I inflicted upon you was unforgivable and if you make that decision I'll honour it. Neither you nor Alys will ever be bothered by me again.' His jaw tightened. 'Alys will always be my daughter and she'll never want for anything. I'll support you both gladly, but I can't go on seeing you, knowing that you can never be mine. If that means losing Alys, well, so be it.'

He was shaking, she realised, and she put her arms around him. 'But I don't think you'll make me go away, my darling. Because I remember what you said when I asked you if you loved Alys's father.'

'With all my heart, until the day I die.' She gazed at him in a sort of wonder, all the pain dissipated in the love that she was now, at last, able to recognise.

'I won't interfere with what you want to do, Jo. You can work, have your career. I promised you the job of your life to entrap you, keep you close to me for a while. It's still yours if you want it.'

'My career seemed very important once,' she said. 'Come and sit down; I have to explain why.' He stiffened, sensing rejection, but she shook her head. 'It's something you should know.'

He nodded briefly and sat beside her on the sofa. 'What is it?'

'It's a story about a little girl. She

had an older sister — ten years older. There had been other babies in between, you understand, but none of them had made it to full term until she arrived and the doctors told her parents that there could be no more babies after that.'

He drew in a sharp breath, but she kept going. It was important that he understand. He had the right to understand.

'The father was sad,' she went on, 'because he could never have the son he wanted so much to follow in his footsteps. So the mother encouraged the little girl in a game. She could take the place of Daddy's son, she told her.'

Clay moved to hold her, but she kept him at bay. 'She didn't mind,' she assured him. 'It was fun. She wore jeans all the time and when she had to wear glasses and braces it didn't matter so much, because boys didn't care about things like that.'

'Jo — '

'Fortunately she was clever, and

because she competed with the boys at school she shone at the things boys were good at — maths and science.' She smiled slightly. 'She wanted so much to make up to her father for not being a boy. And it was easy enough. She would do exactly what a son would: follow her father into his profession. Show him that it didn't matter . . . ' She was surprised by a sudden sob.

He held her then. 'My darling, please don't go on. I think I understand.'

'It's all right, Clay.' She smiled brilliantly through a film of tears. 'Because she passed all her exams. Graduated. She made it. Became a civil engineer, just like her father. He thought it rather amusing and I think . . . I think he was proud. But then he died and I had to try so much harder to make it up to him — ' She broke off, no longer able to speak, and he cradled her until the sobs finally subsided and she was at rest in his arms.

'Did he know what you were trying to do?'

She shook her head. 'I don't think it ever crossed his mind. I was just his funny little tomboy. Mum . . . well, she never discouraged me.'

'Oh, God. And I didn't understand. I just thought you didn't care about me, only about your damned job.'

'I should have told you.'

'Did I ever give you the chance? I just blazed away, my male ego bruised and hurting.' He fetched her a brandy. 'Drink this, slowly.' He watched her as she sipped, gasping at the unexpected heat at the back of her throat. 'Do you want to carry on, my love — working?'

'I don't think I'm much good at anything else.'

'You must do exactly what you want.'

'I don't know what I want. Except . . . ' She turned to face him. 'Except I want to go home, with you. If you still want me.'

10

'Want you?' Clay took her face between his hands and for a long, heart-stopping moment his eyes seemed to devour her. Then, so slowly that Jo had time to rediscover every feature, remind herself of every tiny line and scar on his well-loved, weather-beaten face, he bent to kiss her.

Gently, tenderly, his mouth touched her eyelids, moved to graze the delicate skin at her temples, before taking a diversion to tease the sensitive whorls of her ears. He took all the time in the world, setting her skin ablaze with an answering desire as his lips continued their intoxicating journey across her throat, playing havoc with her heartbeat until the blood was thundering in her ears and she could no longer bear the agony of waiting.

Her lips parted on a soft moan and

finally he took pity on her and accepted the invitation of her tongue, his kiss a sweet, wondrous evocation of their love.

It was a long time before he released her, holding her away from him so that he could see her face. 'Does that answer your question?'

His voice stroked her and Jo simply nodded, unable to speak for sheer happiness. Clay folded her in his arms, holding her close. 'Then we'd better make some important decisions.'

She raised her eyes. 'Decisions?' she asked, her pulse quickening nervously as she saw the intensity with which he regarded her. 'What about?'

'The most important, darling, is where in the world you would like me to take you for your honeymoon.'

'There's no need,' she murmured, and smiled happily. 'I know how busy you are. I shall be perfectly happy just to . . . begin again.'

'And so we will. But I shall never be too busy for you again, Joanna. Never.' He rubbed his cheek against her hair.

'And besides, the decorators won't finish the nursery for at least ten days. You don't expect me to wait that long?'

She sat up. 'Decorators!' She stared at him. 'You never even considered that I would say no! Of all the conceited — '

He caught her waist and pulled her hard against him. ' "With all my heart, until the day I die" . . . ' he softly quoted her, before kissing her again. 'Do you want to change your mind?' he offered at last.

She shook her head. 'No,' she said softly. 'I don't want to change my mind.'

He smiled. 'Well, now that's settled, where would you like to go?'

'I don't know.' She thought for a moment. 'It's too late for beaches and too early for winter sports. Maybe we should wait for a while. Until the summer, perhaps?'

'You're not listening to me, Jo,' he said. 'We're going away for a couple of weeks at least. If nothing else, it will give everyone time to get used to the idea. And when I asked 'where in the world', I did mean just that. There's the Far East. South America. Australia.'

Her eyes flew open. 'That far?'

'Anywhere in the world you would like to go. Just say the word.'

'Anywhere?' Her lips curved into a dreamy smile.

'Anywhere,' he repeated.

'In that case, my love, I think I should like to spend my honeymoon on a desert island.'

His smile was wolfish. 'A real desert island? Or one with a few home comforts?'

She considered for a moment. 'I think I'd like a few home comforts.'

'Perhaps that's just as well, because I give you due warning — I have no intention of wasting any time spearing fish.'

★ ★ ★

The Maldives were everything that Jo had asked for and more. For two weeks they swam and sailed and made love as if they were the last two people on earth.

'It's back to reality tomorrow. Will you mind?' Clay asked as they took a last stroll along the beach.

'No. It's been wonderful. But the truth is that it would have been wonderful anywhere with you.'

'Flatterer.' He kissed her ear. 'And you're missing Alys.' She started guiltily, but he was reassuring. 'It's all right, Jo. I miss her too. I can hardly wait to get back and start to be part of a real family.'

'I'll remind you of that when she wakes up in the middle of the night wanting a drink,' she said, with feeling. She glanced at him sideways from under long dark lashes, hesitating to mention what was on her mind.

'Yes?'

He seemed to have the power to read her mind. 'I'm not looking forward to going back to the office. I shall feel like an exhibit at a waxworks. Everyone will stare when we both come back on the same day with these wonderful matching tans.'

'I briefed my directors before I left. They had a right to know the truth before any silly rumours started to fly about when we disappeared at the same time. Especially since I rather gave the game away with that damned basket of roses. I had Lloyd's resignation on my desk within the hour.' He glanced at her. 'I told him there was no need but I think he'll go anyway.' He stopped and pulled her to him. 'You may rest assured that everyone knows that you're a respectable married lady, and always have been. Now, I think we've walked quite far enough. And talked quite enough. This is our last night in paradise and I don't intend to waste a second of it.'

* * *

'What shall I put on this branch?'
Jo handed Clay a little wooden doll.

'This should look about right. And I think that's enough. If you hang any more ornaments on that tree it will sink through the floor.' She handed him the angel. 'There's just this for the top.'

He placed the angel on the top and turned on the lights. They stepped back in order to judge the effect.

'It's wonderful, Clay. I can't wait for Alys to see it tomorrow. She was too young last Christmas to understand.'

He looped his arm around her waist. 'I only wish — '

'No!' She swivelled in his arms and placed her hand over his mouth. 'Don't say it. Don't waste one second on regret. We have the rest of our lives together and that's what matters.'

'You're right, Mrs Thackeray. And I have an early Christmas present for you.'

He bent and lifted a long package from among the piles of gaily wrapped presents waiting for the morning. 'Happy Christmas.'

She took it from him, turning it in

her hands. 'What is it?'

'Why don't you open it, my darling, and find out?'

Slowly she slipped the ribbons and opened up the wrapping. 'A newspaper?' She looked at him. 'Is this a joke?'

'It's today's edition of *The Times*. Try the personal column and judge for yourself.'

And suddenly she knew. 'Clay! You didn't!'

'I made you a promise.'

She laughed. 'Oh, Clay!' She quickly opened the paper at the page and then she stopped laughing. He had taken an entire page. Filled it with the words.

I love you, Joanna Thackeray. With all my heart, until the day I die. Clay.

A damp spot appeared on the page, then another. She looked up at him through glistening lashes. 'I've never cried for happiness before,' she said, her voice hardly reaching a whisper.

'I recommend that everyone should do it at least once,' he said, gravely.

'Thank you. I believe it's the best

present I've ever had.' She wiped at the tears with her fingers. 'And I have something for you. I was going to wait until tomorrow to give it to you, but I think you should have it now. It seems the right moment, somehow.'

She untied an envelope from the tree and gave it to him. For a moment he held it between his fingers, then pulled the bright red ribbon that fastened it and drew out a sheet of notepaper.

His eyes narrowed. 'What is this?' he asked.

'You'd better read it and see.'

He flicked the paper open and studied it for a moment, his face darkening as he read the words. 'Why are you doing this?' he demanded.

Shaken by his reaction, her voice trembled. 'I thought you would be pleased.'

'And I thought I made it clear that I don't want you doing anything, anything at all, just to please me. You have a great career ahead of you. You'll be regretting this gesture in a month and blame me.' He dropped her letter of resignation to the floor and moved to the table to pour himself a drink. He turned to her. 'Can I get you something?'

She shook her head, unable to for the moment speak.

'I'll open some wine if you'd prefer?'

'No, I won't have anything. I've given it up for a while.'

He poured himself a Scotch. 'Given it up? Why?' Then he swung round and stared at her. 'You're not ill?' His eyes fell on her letter and he went white.

'Is that the reason — ?'

'No, my love. I'm not ill. But you did once say that climbing up and down ladders when you're pregnant is one of the drawbacks of the job.'

'Pregnant!' He was by her side in a stride and seized her by the arms. 'You're pregnant?'

'Are you angry?'

'Angry? Why the hell would I be angry?'

'It's just that you're shouting,' she

said, quietly. 'And you're rather hurting me.'

He looked down in surprise and abruptly released her. Then he grabbed her again, pulling her into his arms. 'Oh, dear God, I'm sorry, Jo. It's all my fault.'

She tilted her head back until she could see his face. 'Certainly it's your fault,' she told him severely. Then a smile lit her beautiful grey eyes. 'Who else's fault could it possibly be? But don't be sorry, Clay Thackeray. Don't ever be sorry. Because I'm not. I couldn't be happier.'

'You're sure?' He shook his head in an effort to think more clearly. 'We could have a nanny. You could still have your — '

'My career? No, my darling. Please understand. I've already missed too much time with Alys. That couldn't be helped; I was lucky to be able to work as I did. But there is nothing of the noble gesture about my resignation. I've simply decided that it's time for a new career.' She slid her hands around his neck. 'Wife and mother will do me just fine from now on.'

'Is that a fact?' His eyes gleamed darkly. 'In that case, Mrs Thackeray, I think you'd better start practising. After all, you've a considerable amount of 'wifing' to catch up on.'

'I'll need a little help with that part of my career plan,' she said.

He swept her up into his arms. 'That, Mrs Thackeray, is no problem. You'll get all the help you'll ever need from me. And I believe we should start right now.'

THE END

We do hope that you have enjoyed reading this large print book.

Did you know that all of our titles are available for purchase?

We publish a wide range of high quality large print books including:
Romances, Mysteries, Classics
General Fiction
Non Fiction and Westerns

Special interest titles available in large print are:
The Little Oxford Dictionary
Music Book, Song Book
Hymn Book, Service Book

Also available from us courtesy of Oxford University Press:
Young Readers' Dictionary
(large print edition)
Young Readers' Thesaurus
(large print edition)

For further information or a free brochure, please contact us at:
Ulverscroft Large Print Books Ltd.,
The Green, Bradgate Road, Anstey,
Leicester, LE7 7FU, England.
Tel: (00 44) **0116 236 4325**
Fax: (00 44) **0116 234 0205**

TROPICAL NIGHTS

Phyllis Humphrey

Tracy Barnes has a few words for real-estate mogul Gregory Thompson. Infuriating. Obstinate. Presumptuous. He's bought the Hawaiian hotel where she works as assistant manager and she could be forced out of her job. If it wasn't for his charm she'd hate him. But Gregory, confident in his ability to win over the guarded Tracy, plans dinner, dancing, and a moonlit walk. Maybe it's Hawaii, but Gregory hasn't felt this good in years . . . or wanted a woman this badly . . .